Brak the Barbarian

John Jakes

BOOK ONE IN THE
BRAK THE BARBARIAN SERIES

Pulp Hero Press
The Most Dangerous Books on Earth
www.PulpHeroPress.com

Pulp Hero Press publishes its books in a variety of print and electronic formats. Some content that appears in one format may not appear in another.

Editor: Bob McLain
Layout: Artisanal Text

ISBN 978-1-68390-293-5
Printed in the United States of America

Pulp Hero Press | **www.PulpHeroPress.com**
Address queries to bob@pulpheropress.com

This book is for my son, Michael

I have wrought my simple plan
If I give one hour of joy
To the boy who's half a man
Or the man who's half a boy.

—A. Conan Doyle

Contents

Brak's World
HIGH STEPPES
SHRINE OF KAGGOTH
KAMBDA KAI
MOUNTAINS OF SMOKE
TOCT
TAZIMS LAND
KOPT
GAT
CHAMBALOR
PHRIXOS
JOVIS
GREAT TYROS
LESSER TYROS
SEA OF CHAM
PILLARS of EBON
LOGOL
QURAN
TIMBELLO
GREAT KOPT
SAMARIND
STRANN'S REALM
N W E S
CITY of the MIRKANS
DARK SEA
KINGDOM of the TWO BAYS
FORREST OF POM
THENNGIL
KINGDOM OF
TOBOOL
KHURDISAN
LORD MAGNUS

Author's Original Preface

When the first Brak tale saw print, its appearance was followed shortly by a letter to the magazine that had published it. I have lost my copy of the letter since, but I recall its inferences quite clearly—and painful ones they were for an author.

The reader's letter expressed the opinions that Brak was but a pale ghost of mighty Conan and, what was worse, had probably been conceived either out of ignorance of Conan, or with full knowledge and therefore out of sheer cupidity.

To the first part of the charge I plead delightedly guilty. That teller of marvelous tales, Robert Howard, did indeed create a giant in whose shadow other "hero tales" must stand and sometimes, admittedly, suffer.

But be ignorant of all of his work?

Or believe that readers would be hoodwinked, and not feel the pulse of common blood which riots through all the warriors who inhabit the world of sword and sorcery?

No.

My motive for giving birth to Brak and his parallel universe on an old black iron Underwood was much simpler. There just are not enough stories of this kind to go around any more; not enough, anyway, to please me.

To help fill this dismal gap well or badly—I hope never indifferently—my barbarian, with the long yellow braid and the light of the south horizons glittering in his eyes, was born.

—John Jakes
Brighton, New York / Kettering, Ohio
1961-1967

Diamonds in the caravans.
Pennons on the plain.
Yellow fog and slime-red hands
Within a wizard's fane.

Horse dung in the palace yard.
Wenches plump and fair.
Dead who travel. Daggers bared.
Pits that belch and glare.

Rascals in the market place.
Magii round the throne.
Gryphon hulls and spires of pearl.
Iron, amber, stone.

Clanging steel and capon lords.
Rubies flung in mud.
*Unfurl the darkling splendours—
I sing the Age of Blood!*

PART ONE

The Unspeakable Shrine

The stars are trailing clouds of sin
While heroes drowse and dream.
As temples crack and tumble in,
Mad holy men blaspheme.
Behold the soul's dark night begin—
Yob-Haggoth rules supreme!

—The Vision of Nestoriamus

"God is dead!"

Tittering and drooling, the craze-eyed mendicant rattled his copper bowl and blocked the narrow street. Filthy hair hung to his shoulders. His teeth were rotted brown stumps. Gaining no immediate response from the huge, brawny barbarian whom he had chosen to stop and importune, the mendicant whined all the more insistently.

"God is dead, the abominations be praised! A dinsha for this most deserving and humble of the Dark One's spawn...

"A coin?" said the barbarian. "Beg elsewhere."

"One coin only, barbarian."

"Get away from me."

"Only one, lord and master..."

"I said get away."

A gigantic nausea filled the belly of the strapping stranger whose way the mendicant blocked. Smells of offal, of drugs, sweet sputtering torchwood, narrow thoroughfares that still managed to exude a stink despite the crispness of the frosty air, all mingled together in the nostrils of the big man, making him want to choke, or curse, or both.

He had walked through the wall gate of Kambda Kai at chill sunset and had been wandering wonderstruck in its riotous streets for the better part of this night. Everywhere he had seen nothing but squalor, sharp practices, licentiousness. If this were the dazzle of the great civilized kingdoms that lay between him and fabled Khurdisan, then he had erred in taking the southern road out of the high steppes, the wild lands of the north.

The mendicant refused to be put off: "Just one lowly dinsha, outlander. One poor coin, and in return I will direct thee to a certain house where most delicious spectacles are performed in honor of the Dark One, Yob-Haggoth, who has banished the Nameless God. If you but know the correct word to tell the doorkeeper in that house, you will see amazing things, such as enchanted hill goats, and young, plump maidens who turn into..."

"I have no taste for that kind of depravity," growled the barbarian. His right hand dropped toward the haft of the huge broadsword at his waist. "Stand out of my path."

The mendicant's eyes flickered. He glanced right and left, as though seeking assistance. The narrow way of frowzy shops was quiet. Just ahead, where the street became a slop-strewn stair and rose half the height of a house-storey, revellers could be seen on the upper level. They raced back and forth across a square under the frosted blue light of links hung in walls.

Said the mendicant, "It's clear you don't have the proper respect for citizens of the Ice-marches, friend. A foolish attitude. Most foolish."

"I know nothing of this country you call the Ice-marches," replied the barbarian. "Nor do I believe I want to know more. I am passing through on a journey. Now will you let me by?"

So saying, he withdrew the broadsword from its plain beaten scabbard just enough so that the mendicant flinched backward a step, uncertain as to whether the barbarian meant to draw it out fully and gut him. The big stranger's lips skinned back over his white teeth and with a ghoulishly friendly smile he added: "If you do mean to balk me in my journey, beggar, say out plainly. Then we shall see what can be done to change your mind."

The mendicant muttered epithets in an unfamiliar tongue. But a rumbling laugh built within the brawny chest of the barbarian, for he had worked round a step or two so that the scrofulous beggar was now backed against a shadow-stepped corner between intersecting walls.

The mendicant seemed to hunch in fright, cowed by the figure before him: the bigger man plainly was an outlander, a huge, yellow-headed giant whose hair was plaited in a single long braid that hung down his back. A glossy fur cloak and cowl around the barbarian's shoulders reflected the torch glare dimly. The big man was naked save for this fur and a garment of lion's hide about his hips.

The tense scene held a moment longer, the barbarian in a wide-legged stance that indicated he was ready for the worst. The mendicant's face changed. It became fawning.

"May Yob-Haggoth smooth my tongue for the proper apologies," he whined. "I did not recognize in your honor a man of such stout purpose. Of course you are free to go on your way. I will seek out another newcomer to the city of Kambda Kai to fill my humble bowl."

With those words he raised his beggar's cup, as though to show it to the barbarian. But in so doing, he suddenly cackled with laughter, snapping his wrist hard.

Coins flew. The dinshas struck the barbarian's cheeks and eyes, startling him. The mendicant squealed and darted around him, strident breath clouding in the sharp night air. The barbarian spun as the mendicant raced toward the stairs at the street's end and let out a high-pitched cry: "We'll see how arrogant you are with the magical blind boys, clod." Waving his arms, he howled, "Ho, Darters! Ho, down here in Sweetmeat Alley. Ho, a stranger!"

And in the blowing murk at the top of the stairs, a company of small, lithe figures who had been racing past wheeled into sight.

The yellow-headed barbarian slid over so that his back was against the wall of a building along the street. In an upper window across the way, a young girl looked out, sleepy-mouthed, dream-eyed. She noticed the uproar below as the dozen or more filthy boys screeched and squealed down the stairs. Raising a drug pipe to her pink lips, she turned away inside, indifferent. In the night there was the beat of timbrels, the clap of hands, the shriek of mindless laughing.

Since leaving the high steppes and coming down through the foothills across the border of this craggy land known as the Ice-marches, the barbarian had encountered no civilized places until he reached the walls of Kambda Kai. At first it had seemed a splendid city. But now, from all appearances, civilization was turning out to be little more than thievery, blasphemy and other depraved occupations. And it further appeared that he would be forced to fight a pack of children.

The boys formed a half-circle just up the street. They were ragtag, underfed, dirty-skinned waifs with straggly hair and pointed wolf's teeth. The big barbarian noticed with a start that something was amiss in their faces.

Where eyepits should have been, each boy carried two silver-crystal disks somehow embedded between eyebrow and cheekbone. Their fingertips, too, were made of this silver-crystal stuff, pointed, like needles.

"Our little acolytes of Yob-Haggoth," the mendicant spat, "are most efficient when it comes to disposing of outlanders who mock the Dark One's ways. At him, Darters!"

A boy somewhat taller than the rest stepped forward. The blind silver-crystal disks shone and winked with reflections of the smoky blue torches round about. The boy capered, a vaguely frightening little figure in his animal-skin breech clout. He executed a contemptuous bow.

"Honorable greetings, outlander," he piped. "Blessings on you and welcome to Kambda Kai, capital of the Ice-marches. A difficulty here?"

"One was just concluded," the barbarian rumbled, "and another is about to begin if you mean to quarrel. Be off, little boy, before I take this sword and whack your backside."

The Darter's pointed teeth glittered. Others in his company stirred, hopping from foot to foot, making an ominous hiss between their teeth. The silver-crystal disks of their eyes shone with strange luminescence. The barbarian's spine crawled.

That he, a grown man, should be forced to confront such a pack of underfed striplings somehow did not seem amusing. Rather, it seemed ominous. There was a sensation of great menace pressing near.

Perhaps it was the strangeness of this city, which he had expected to be so full of wonders. It was the first city he had ever entered in all his savage life. It had turned out to be a place of deceit, of shadows, of the sense of vileness whispering behind a thousand latticed, dark-lit doorways.

"We will forgive your crude tongue, outlander," said the boy, clicking his silver-needle fingertips together, "if you will answer but a question or two."

The big barbarian quickly decided it was better to delay them with talk than to launch against them with his blade.

The notion of swinging his broadsword at a company of children still did not sit well in his belly.

"Speak on," he rumbled.

"From where do you come?" the boy inquired, bobbing his head forward as if to listen closely.

"From the north."

"Where are you bound?"

"Into the south."

"Have you a name?"

"Among my people I'm called Brak."

He did not feel it was necessary to mention that he had been cast out by those people, cast out by his own kind. Yet even before that dark event, he had already decided to leave, for he had heard from a wandering shaman about the strange, rich, warm lands that lay southward. He had mocked the war-like gods of his own kind once too often, and had been banished, he set out.

His banishment was not entirely grim. He had a destination.

He was bound to seek his fortune in the warm climes of Khurdisan far southward, and was ready to be dazzled by the splendors of the cities and kingdoms which, the shaman said, lay between. He was ready to fight his way, if necessary, until he came to the great crescent-shaped land of Khurdisan that stretched, so the shaman told, nearly from the Pillars of Ebon in the west to the Mountains of Smoke where the world ended in the east.

Khurdisan. Khurdisan the golden. The name was music, and his constant companion. In Khurdisan, the shaman said, there was plunder, fat plunder for the taking. And golden sunlight, and gold-skinned girls.

And this was how, in a jingling, blue-lit street in Kambda Kai, hardly started on his quest, Brak the barbarian found himself already balked, face to face with a company of weirdlings who hissed between pointed teeth.

"One question more, Brak," the Darter boy said with another click of his silver-needle nails. "What god calls you to his throne?"

"I have been told there are many gods in the kingdoms between here and the south," Brak answered. "In this I find confusion. I know none of them. I bow to none."

With a malevolent little snarl, the Darter boy rushed close, his blind-eyed face upturned. "There is no god but Yob-Haggoth, outlander. We are his people. One of the needle-like-fingers waggled under Brak's nose. "If you will but fall to your knees and vow fealty to Yob-Haggoth who rules not only the Ice-marches but all the world, you may pass on."

Brak's pulses quickened with a fury. "I told you I bow down to no one, spindle-legs."

"Yob-Haggoth is supreme! Yob-Haggoth casts his dark and blessed mantle over all the world. Yea, over those who claim him and over those who do not. He vanquished the Nameless God in times gone by, and he is the king of all the good darkness. You *will* swear fealty to him."

Brak's patience had worn thin. He lifted his strong right hand and placed the palm against the forehead of the filthy-haired Darter boy, intending to thrust him away.

Just as his palm made contact, a ghastly tingling began, a sharp, stabbing pain which lanced upward into his shoulder and made him reel back panting against the wall.

The silver-crystal disks in the Darter boy's face glittered as he danced away. He laughed: "Ho, mates! I think we've found our mystical third this night. One believer—one who worships the Nameless God—and now this outlander, black in his unbelief. Before the sun rises, three bloods can mingle in praise of Yob-Haggoth."

Through this indecipherable harangue, Brak stood tensely, still agonized by the pain in his forearm. He tried to flex his fingers so that he might pull his broadsword free. The Darter boys were closer now, shuffling forward in a closing semicircle, uttering those foul hisses between their teeth. The boy whom Brak had touched raised his fingers, pointed, cried: "Take him, lads. Take him for the glory of the Dark One."

The Darters charged forward, blind eyes flashing.

Instantly Brak summoned what little strength was left in his right arm and hauled out his broadsword. The time for scruples had passed. The mighty iron blade winked out. In the narrow street, a deadly silence fell.

From the square at the top of the stairs at street's end, women cried out in abandon. Brak had a dim vision of a young girl sprawled prone and protesting on the back of a he-goat that was dragged along by a rope, the rope in turn being pulled by half-a-dozen revellers who filled the night with licentious howls. The evil sight was quickly obscured in the blowing smoke, but somehow Brak knew that the entire vile tissue of this city of Kambda Kai periled him now.

The Darters shuffled forward. They hissed, their silver-disk eyes glowing. Swallowing, Brak hefted his broadsword. He grasped its hilt with both hands to swing it around in front of him and hew a path free.

With an abrupt cry, the leader of the Darters leaped high in the air. He grasped a beam that projected from the storey of the house over Brak's head. The boy hung there, mewing and laughing and waving one arm to direct his fellows forward. Brak took a lunging step. Somewhere the mendicant laughed with revengeful pleasure. Brak swung the broadsword with all his might.

Up flew the hands of the Darter boys. From the tips of their silver-nail fingers, tiny spurts of silver light hissed through the air.

One molten droplet struck Brak's arcing blade and exploded with a shower of green and crimson sparks. Another stung against his shoulder, made him clench his teeth at sudden, violent pain.

He hacked the broadsword back and forth through the air, but it was suddenly enveloped by a rainstorm of those silver darts. Touching his blade, each burst into a star shower of sparks. Soon his vision was blinded by a phantasmal curtain of light beyond which he could not see.

Other droplets of the silver stuff pricked against his skin, bringing exquisite agony at every contact. Brak flung back his head, howling with savage fury.

The red tide of anger ran high in him now. He dropped his broadsword with a clang. He flung off his fur cloak and cowl, the better to maneuver. He bent down to retrieve the sword and stared into a dazzle of sparks that grew brighter, *brighter*, so bright that he could barely see the dimly glittering haft of his great weapon.

At last his fingers closed around it. The blade felt as heavy as the heaviest metal when he struggled to lift it.

The increasing rain of silver darts drove him back along the wall. He raged and cursed and yelled in his barbaric tongue, swinging his broadsword into the firestorm of exploding sparks which continued to spurt from the needle-fingers of the Darter boys. Dimly he sensed them closing in around him. He saw flashes of silver-disk eyes through the exploding patterns of light.

He was being crowded back and back, driven along the wall of the street like a goaded animal in a pen. Each time he swung the sword with his pain-lanced arms, it cut through nothing at all but more coruscations of fire. Rising in the noisy night of Kambda Kai he heard the hissing laughter.

All at once something hard gave beneath his straining back.

Turning, Brak staggered into what appeared to be a courtyard. He felt paving stones beneath his feet. He blundered ahead, eyes still smarting with the painful reflections of the darts of the boys. He nearly toppled into a scum-covered pool where a fish's skeleton bobbed.

Struggling to keep his senses, he whirled back around in a split second, lunged, and threw his mighty shoulder against the great basswood door that had opened in the wall. One of the Darter boys was just charging through. The slam of the door caught the boy by surprise. He shrieked.

Brak shouldered the door all the way shut. It would not close completely, for the Darter boy's right hand was thrust through the opening. The hand blazed with silver darts that shot away and illuminated the courtyard.

Brak steeled himself with the thought that these were not children but savage, magical creatures in children's form. He raised his sword arm while still leaning against the door. Mercilessly he chopped downward.

The Darter boy's arm was lopped off. No blood gouted, only a foul-smelling puff of saffron smoke.

From the street came furious hisses and a single insane bleat of pain. Brak was able to shut the door fully with one more mighty heave of his shoulder. He rammed the bolt into its socket.

Panting, his whole body tormented by the stings of the darts which had touched him, he closed his eyes and rested briefly against the rough door.

What madness was this? he wondered. How foul were these so-called civilizations, these fabled kingdoms and cities of men into which he had chosen to wander in quest of fortune? What pit-born demons haunted the world? All at once he bitterly regretted the circumstances that had driven him from the high steppes. He cursed the decision to bow to that fate and journey south.

But in a moment, his basically simple nature reasserted itself, and he realized he had no choice but to go forward. Taking a tighter grip on his broadsword, he started across the courtyard.

It was lit dimly by the reflections of the icy northern stars high up in the velvet-dark sky. He must seek a way out of this house, this city.

From the street the savage hisses continued. Brak circled the rot-crusted pool. He was half way to the interior wall of the house when a strange, pearl-clouded light sprang up ahead of him. Doors seemed to swing open in the house wall. He was bedazzled.

There stood a girl of incredible beauty. Midnight-colored silks clung to her body. Her eyes were equally dark, and black hair floated like a cloud around her. She smiled with plum lips that glistened moist in her lovely white face.

What new devil's snare was this? Brak asked himself. The pearl cloud seemed to hover about her as she stood with hands on the ornamental copperwork of the doors into the house. Brak guessed she had opened the doors from within, spilling out the pearl light. Yet he could not remember having actually seen the doors open.

His head throbbed. His body ached with the stings of the Darters. Overhead, the very stars seemed to whirl and pitch.

"Here is the way, outlander," the girl said with a sweet smile.

Hope surged within Brak. Her beauty was incredible. Perhaps he had found a kindly stranger in this den of wickedness at last. Wiping his mouth with his forearm, he bobbed his head to signal that he had heard. He started toward her, toward those doors into the house where he could discern no features, only a pearl brightness.

From behind the girl's ebon robes a head covered with ringlets popped out. Silver-disk eyes glared.

Brak stopped, thunderstruck. The leader of the Darters pranced out from where he had been hiding behind the girl.

He chirruped at her: "A splendid ploy! Oh, splendid, my pretty Daughter of Hell." And he raised his needle-fingers to point at Brak's face.

"Gulled!" Brak cried, dragging up his broadsword.

"Aye, barbarian," smiled the girl, her black eyes brighter now, bright but cold as stones from the earth's chillest place. "The Darters summoned me here from a great way off because the mystical triad must be presented on Yob-Haggoth's altar before the sun rises. His power must be renewed."

The voice that had sounded so sweetly just moments ago was sweet still, yet now it was full of hidden subtleties, as though spiders crawled in her throat, spiders and other foul things that she relished. The Darter boy could hardly contain his glee. He capered from one dirty foot to the other: "Shall I take him, Ariane? Shall I, shall I?"

"Yes, and quickly. The stars are falling. My father's voice calls in my ears. We must haste."

"Foul pit-things!" Brak shouted, raising his broadsword and charging forward to gut them.

The Darter boy's silver-needle fingers flashed and flared with a new intensity. A hundred, a thousand spurts of light engulfed Brak. They battered him, pierced into his very skull to drive him senseless with pain.

He struggled to maintain a grip on his broadsword. He could not. He felt his immense legs wavering, turning flabby. Slowly, slowly, he fell spiraling through a fire-coruscating dark toward the paving stones, leagues away.

As he fell he twisted around. Through the spurt and flare of needles from the hands of the hissing Darter boy, he saw something else that filled him with horror and set his mind to wailing with silent despair.

The depth of their evil magic revealed itself. Where there had been a splintery basswood door in the high street wall, a door through which he had escaped into this demon's courtyard, there was no door now. Brak saw only unblemished stone. In a red burst of delirium, Brak sank down and knew nothing else.

There was a passage underneath the stars, Brak waking briefly to dream or imagine himself lashed belly down over the reeking hide of a snow camel. Its cloven hoofs struck phosphorescent yellow sparks from the frozen slate of the Ice-marches countryside. Darter boys ran alongside. They chittered and chirruped among themselves, their huge diskeyes upturned to catch the reflections of the lost, mournful stars.

And then all this blurred away, like a mirror whose surface has been dashed over with scented oil. Brak's pain increased again.

Another time he waked to imagine himself lying on his back, cold upon damp paving stones. His blurred vision focused somewhere high above.

He perceived arched stonework, mammoth ceiling blocks webbed with something like a spider's lacy spinning. But this scarlet-colored web was immensely thick in each strand, and dripped a viscous, reddish fluid that fell plip-plop on the paving stones near his cheek. The fallen drops sent up a stench such as he had never smelled in his lifetime.

For a long moment, as his vision dimmed and cleared, dimmed and cleared, he stared up in hideous fascination at the undulating web affixed to the ceiling. Under a far arch, the web's inhabitant stirred.

Two faceted sullen red eyes blinked open in the thick shadows up there. For a moment Brak's vision was sharp enough to pick out an image duplicated within every one of the facets of the eyes; a human shape, without garments, but apparently sexless. The shape writhed and gesticulated as though being roasted in the hottest of fires. Each incredible twist and turn of suffering was multiplied ten, a hundred, a thousand times inside each of the red facets of the web-dweller's eyes.

Nearby, human voices muttered. Brak tried to turn his head, but could not. A cold, musty draught played across his bare chest. He could recognize walls, the walls of the dim chamber, far away at the limits of his vision. The walls shimmered with reddish reflections, as though somewhere in the vast hall a fire flickered, holding back the dark that pulsed with some nameless evil.

Somehow Brak knew it was an evil older and more foul than all the evil that had ever gone before.

Suddenly, the red watcher's eyes vanished, up there among the cables of the web. No, they merely dulled, Brak realized. A puzzling opalescent screen had come between him and the webbing.

This turned out to be a huge, shimmering bubble, black at the perimeter, misty gray in the center. The bubble was descending into his line of vision.

Twice as tall as a man, this hovering bubble contained a human figure. Brak's throat clogged with a vestigial growl. The figure in the bubble belonged to the girl of the midnight-hued silks and robes, Ariane.

Her plum-red lips twisted in a little smile of interest. Brak somehow understood that from her mystical vantage point within the bubble, floating there twice human size, she could survey him.

In her chalk-white face her eyes burned with a luster of unnatural curiosity. He struggled to rise. Nausea swept over him.

The bubble dropped nearer. Within it Ariane stirred, her hair floating slowly, slowly back and forth behind her, as though she swam undersea. She lifted her right hand. She brought her curved nails to her lips and blew a kiss.

Her eyes lusted bright and strange. Down her wrists ran tiny red threads of fresh blood. Blood, Brak sensed, that was not hers, not hers… Ariane smiled and smiled, tempting him with those plum-ripe lips, tempting him, *beckoning him.*

Brak shuddered, went rigid. His eyes filmed over. His head began to pound once more, and he shivered in the grip of a nameless sickening fear.

The bubble floated up and away. Ariane's figure diminished. Brak bit into his lower lip and moaned. Icy sweat bathed him.

Muted male voices which he had heard briefly at the start of the feverish interlude whispered again.

"Who, who? I cannot see."

"Doesn't the crawling of your flesh tell you?" This second voice was hoarse, strained. "*His* daughter. She is curious about him, the stranger. And admiring of his strength, I think."

The other voice, older, with a quaver in it, came again: "But dawn comes on, friar! There is no time for her to take him to her arms."

"Do you not understand her powers, old one? That foul bitch can stretch one beat of my heart into eons with her magic. In that time she can claim a thousand lovers, or only one, and make each wish afterward that he had perished in his mother's womb."

Overhead the reddened spider-like eyes with their multifaceted images of a human creature writhing in torment slowly closed. The last voice, located some-where out along the paving-stone floor beyond Brak's line of vision, murmured on: "If Ariane is interested in the outlander, old one, then when the ritual ceremony commences at first light, he will not have a soul as big as an olive seed left for Yob-Haggoth to gobble up."

The voice receded. Brak wondered with dull horror what would happen to him, now that he had roused the curiosity of the bubble-locked witch. *He must rise up.*

Powerless, he felt pain sweep through him again. He gave a mighty groan. His head lolled to one side. Fire danced up the walls of the gigantic chamber. He knew no more.

The last wakening was sudden.

Reality was the chill, hard touch of stone under his naked spine. The lion's tail of his clout lumped under his buttocks. His eyes flicked wide and he knew the enchantment had worn off.

A raw gurgle of curiosity coursed up in Brak's throat. Standing above him, limned against the background he had seen before (distant walls, the web high up dripping its gut-stinking ooze), were two outlandish-looking men.

One wore dirty robes and had a matted beard, flowing mustaches and tangled hair. He might once have been tall and commanding. Age had bent his shoulders. His tongue kept darting back and forth across his cracked old lips. He was blind.

His eyes were slits, the lids sewn tightly down against the flesh of his upper cheeks by means of thick black thread. The thread was partially overgrown with dark scabs and ugly cartilage.

The other person had a less alarming mien, yet he terrified Brak the more. He was a stout, bald man of small stature. He wore a gray cowl and robe, A girdle of beads hung at his waist. In his right hand he held a small cross of pitted gray stone.

The horizontal and vertical arms of this cross were of equal length. The cowled man held it by its lower vertical arm, and was passing the artifact back and forth through the air over Brak's head. The unfamiliar symbol and the feeling that some hideous ceremony was in progress combined to bring Brak leaping to his feet, screaming his rage: "Take that thing from before my eyes, wizard!" His mighty fingers locked around the throat of the cowled man, who began to gasp and squirm in terror.

"He means no harm, he means no harm!" piped the old blind man who had heard the sounds of struggle.

Red madness crested behind Brak's eyes, and he saw closeup the rubicund face of the cowled man. It was a face common, plain, and free of guilt. Brak took his hands from the man's throat and stood back, fists clenching and unclenching at his sides.

The stone cross had fallen to the paving stones. Brak pointed at it.

"I don't know what that thing is, gray robe. But I want no more spells cast on me."

With a peculiar tenderness, the cowled man picked up the artifact. "From where do you come, barbarian?" Then his eyes narrowed as he guessed: "Northward? The steppes?"

Brak's tone was guarded. "Aye."

"Then you have never seen a cross of Nestoriamus."

"Is that what you call the thing? No, I never have. Let me see." He extended his hand. The cowled man closed his fingers protectively. He would not release the artifact.

After a moment the cowled man said, "This is the cross of the Nameless God whose face cannot be seen and whose name must be forever unwritten. I am the protector of this cross. I am a priest of the order of Nestoriamus. I am called Friar Jerome."

Brak grunted and peered around the chamber. The breath of amazement whistled across his lips. As he had sensed in his delirium, the hall was high and wide and deep enough to have held an entire host of warriors. There were no windows, and only one visible door, this a pair of mighty portals five times Brak's own height.

The only illumination in the whole dismal place came from a small sunken pit in the center of the paving-stone floor. There a few beech branches crackled, casting a feeble dancing light on the walls and sending smoke curling into the air. Its tang could not obscure the smell of the red droolings that fell steadily from the web on the ceiling. The droplets stained and even pitted the floor.

"I do not know why I am here," Brak said, advancing toward the fire, "except that I was set upon by enchanters in the city of Kambda Kai, to which I came peacefully." The fire warmed his thick, sword-calloused palms but scantily. A chill mist seemed to suffuse the immense hall. His voice rang hollow as he glowered at the monkish person and the tottering old wreck with the sewn-shut eyes. "Nor do I know who you really are, either of you. And I desire your company not at all."

The Friar raised a pudgy hand. "Peace, outlander. We need not quarrel. We can do naught now but await starset. At the first light of day, the priest of this place will..."

"What place?" Brak demanded, sitting down on the low coping that circled the fire pit. "Is this a tomb? A palace?"

"An idol," whispered the blind old one. "An idol that towers thirty times a man's height. Towers toward the very stars, to blot everything below in darkness." The ancient lips twisted, as though tasting bitter fruit. "This is the northernmost shrine of Yob-Haggoth, barbarian. The greatest of his images in all the known world. From the outside it is an immense statue, with a fearsome visage. It crouches near the borders where the Ice-marches stops and the endless wastes to the north begin."

Now Brak managed a sound faintly resembling a laugh. "Endless wastes? 'Tis where I was born and suckled, old man. Where I lived and fought until they cast me out for mocking their gods. And here I find myself, an innocent pilgrim—" Friar Jerome glanced at Brak's savage shoulders and registered weary skepticism with a lift of a brow. "—an innocent pilgrim within some cursed god's fane, about to be done to death for the gods know what reason. I want no part of these alien rituals!"

The blind man sank down upon the coping beside Brak. "As the Friar said, we can do nothing."

Jerome nodded. "We too were plucked by the Darter boys from the streets of Kambda Kai. We too are prisoners. They will slay us all come dawn, in a rite too loathsome for description." Jerome's eyes grew agonized in the firelight. "The rite is conducted twice in each year. It is the way in which the god Yob-Haggoth transfers his power to him who conducts the rite."

Brak's bleak eyes turn quizzical. "And who is that?"

In a whisper Jerome replied, "Septegundus," and moved the cross in the air.

Brak's spine began to crawl with a foul, cold sweat. The shadows seemed to stir within the vast hall. High above in the dripping scarlet web, the faceted eyes flashed open, revealing again a thousand souls swaying and twisting in torments of posture that were identical, facet to facet.

Septegundus...*Septegundus*. The name rang through Brak like the peal of an immense bell, chilling him with a dread he could not fathom. Suddenly he surged to his feet. He uttered a low, primeval yell. With his yellow braid trailing out behind him, he charged toward the mighty doors and hurled his still-aching frame against them.

They would not give the slightest bit. Brak threw back his head and howled a long, furious animal howl. He beat his fists against the portals until his hands bled. Still he could not budge the great doors.

Finally, beginning to realize the enormity of the horror in which he found himself engulfed, he staggered panting back to the fire pit. There the old one with the sewn-shut eyes regarded the befouled ceiling while one of his sere cheeks jerked in a mad spasm. Friar Jerome shook his head.

"I do not need pity from you!" Brak shouted. "Not from a priest of a catchpenny god!"

Once more Jerome shook his head. "Of the one god, barbarian. The Nameless God."

A queer twitch of fright, of unbelief, of terror at the presence of forces too vast for comprehension filled Brak then. When Jerome signed him to sit once more on the coping, he obeyed.

He chastised himself silently. These men were not enemies but allies. True, he would not have chosen them as fighting companions. Not even as persons with whom to exchange a few words if they passed each other along a mountain trail. But fate had thrust them together, and Brak decided that he should attempt to understand who they were, and what their presence signified.

More calmly he asked: "I do not know your meaning when you talk of the Nameless God or this Yob-Haggoth or—(he was about to pronounce the name *Septegundus*. In his mind a sinister bell boomed, tolled, clanged.) "...or that other."

Friar Jerome nodded, and began to walk back and forth. His sandals slapped softly on stone. "That is because you have come from a far country. To what purpose, may I ask?"

Haltingly Brak told them how he had heard legends of the land of Khurdisan far southward, and had determined that he would journey there to find his fortune. It was all very difficult. He was ill at ease in their presence. He felt that his speech was rude. Furthermore he felt naked. His broadsword had been taken from him.

In a tone of patience similar to that which a father might use to instruct a child, Jerome said, "Your lack of knowledge of this place, this battleground, is understandable, friend Brak. But the shaman told you truly. There are many splendors in the world of man and all of his kingdoms that lie between these far northern reaches and the hot crescent of Khurdisan in the south. There are perils as well. The world is full of many incredible, magical beasts and gods. Most are cruel. Perhaps the cruelest is man himself. Whether man be god or beast, I have never decided."

The words echoed eerily in the empty hall. A twig popped in the pit. Sparks stung Brak's flanks. He brushed them away impatiently. "Help my ignorance, Friar. Tell me about these gods. One of them, I gather, will take all our lives when the sun rises."

"Each kingdom and principality of this world, Brak," Jerome explained with a strange weariness, "is ruled by its own god. Some are powerful, with many spells and wizardries at their command. Yet most mighty of all are two who constantly war for ultimate supremacy in the world. Their presence is for the most part undreamed of by the lords and princes and commoners and magi who keep their eyes focused upon smaller, meaner matters, smaller, meaner gods.

"Centuries in the past, before the Scroll of History was even a little way unrolled, one of these two powerful gods ruled all the world. Yob-Haggoth." Jerome's lips curled, as though the word were filth upon his tongue. "This very monument, as you have heard, is one of his baleful images, a relic of those lost times when he was worshipped publicly in loathsome rites.

"Yob-Haggoth and his worship have been banished these many years. But he has not died. He only slumbers. Of late he had reasserted his power. Perhaps because *this* doctrine—" Jerome's fingers touched the stone cross which he had inserted in the girdle at his waist, "—has gained converts here and there. The world, you see, is a complex and wondrous place. One force frequently begets another counterforce. Until now Yob-Haggoth could slumber undisturbed, for when the lesser wizards perpetrated the evil of the lesser gods, they did the Dark One's work. Perhaps this," again a touching of the cross, "has turned the tide a little, and the Dark One wakes, fearful."

"And this Septegundus," Brak said, forcing himself to pronounce the name, "is a priest of this evil god?"

Jerome gave a nod, a shudder. "Ageless, timeless—some say the mightiest wizard known since creation—that is Septegundus. He is Yob-Haggoth's chief priest and emissary within the world. He is not a man. Yet he is. He dwells in a man's form. But being of his god's essence, he never truly dies. When I was set upon in the city and brought here, I discovered to my horror that he had reappeared. And so it is that we are destined to be offered in the rite which Yob-Haggoth demands twice yearly. The rite will be presided over by Yob-Haggoth's amyr, Septegundus." Pausing, Jerome breathed, "The Amyr of Evil upon Earth."

Bowing his head, Jerome shuddered and made a quick cross-like motion in front of his breast.

Brak pointed again. "And with that mystic cross that you draw on the air you hope to ward him off?"

"Aye. Such is my prayer." Jerome's eyes grew even more somber. "But faith in the Nameless God is never a sinecure, nor even a guarantee against harm.

His followers and priests have been sorely tested in past generations. And in this hour the battle waxes hotter still, for more and more souls turn to Yob-Haggoth, who can gratify their public as well as their private lusts. The world through which you sought to travel, Brak, is a world at war. And my god, who is without a name and without an image, faces the stronger opposition."

When Brak asked an impatient, derisive question concerning the nature of this Nameless God, the Friar did not bridle or grow enraged. Patiently he explained that the Nameless God was a deity who ruled all the world without regard to national boundaries, or so his followers and priests believed. It was a peculiar and puzzling doctrine. Brak had never before heard of gods who crossed native boundaries. Apparently the notion had first been enunciated by a goatherd named Nestoriamus.

May centuries earlier, according to Jerome, the goatherd, founder of the cult, had met his death attempting to carry the Nameless God's symbol, a stone cross, high into the Mountains of Smoke in the dim east, the area in which all gods were presumed to be born and have their seats of power. Nestoriamus vanished. This only confirmed the belief of his family, friends, and neighbors that he was crazed. The strength of his doctrine had waned for a time. But now, Jerome said, there was a small but militant cult of Nestorians abroad in the world once more.

Brak snorted. "We could use a few of them here, armed with iron blades."

Friar Jerome shook his head. "Our strength lies in this." He fingered the cross.

"Not my strength," Brak snarled back. "If there is a door out of this hell, it will only be unlocked by a length of fighting blade."

The Friar's face fell, as though he had been hoping for a less violent denial of his faith. Brak really could not comprehend such theological niceties. He lunged to his feet. He stalked back and forth, his great braid swinging behind his back. At length he spun back to confront Jerome and the old blind man. A drop of the filthy ichor from the ceiling web struck and splattered beside his naked left foot. A bit of it touched his skin, burning painfully. Brak was reminded of the way the hours of the night marched on.

"What exactly is to happen to us at sunrise?" he demanded.

"A ceremony," piped the old one with the sewn eyes. "We die for the glory of Yob-Haggoth."

Now Brak scratched his chin, buffeting his own brains to call up a memory. "In the street where they fell upon me, there was some clack about it. The boys said three persons were necessary...

Blindly plucking at his robes, the elderly man moved closer. His breath smelled of sour wine. "Yes, 'tis the prescribed ritual, outlander. Yob-Haggoth must be offered a threefold death. One death must be the death of a follower of Yob-Haggoth's fiercest foe."

Jerome pushed his cowl back and brushed at his sweating pate. "I am that one."

"They called likewise for an unbeliever," Brak mused. "That is my part?"

The thin-shanked old fellow nodded. "It seems so." Bitterly his cracked lips curled. "I am the third of the triad. I am he who believed. Once I did not, you understand. But in my early manhood I struck a bargain with this selfsame Septegundus. In return for the pledge of my mortal soul to the service of Yob-Haggoth, as well as the tangible sacrifice of my eyes as a token of my good faith..."

"The god blinded you?" Brak breathed.

"Ah, no. It was the daughter of Septegundus who did the deed."

Here Jerome whispered softly, "Ariane. The black-haired one. She came earlier, barbarian. She watched you with curiosity and perhaps with more than that. She is called the Daughter of Hell with good reason. Her beauty is like a festival cake with poison pus under its crust."

"She was as agelessly lovely then as she is now," the old blind man mumbled. "It was Ariane who took the green wands fresh cut from the tree. She sharpened them, and while I lay on the earth, controlling my trembling as best I could—I had agreed to pay the price for what I lusted after, you see—she took the sticks and with tender little motions of her wrists, she impaled both my eyes and put them out. The power of my wits grew after that. For many a year my tongue sang beautiful songs." The silver head bowed and the sewn-shut eyes seemed to twitch as the elderly man added softly, "My name is Tyresias."

Brak blinked. It meant nothing. But Jerome was stunned. "The minstrel? The nightingale mouth who could make a warlord weep?"

Tyresias nodded. "Yes, yes. All the kingdoms of the world flung their gates open to me when I was at the height of my powers. Wine spurted red as life at the courts. Maidens kissed the hem of my silver robe and begged me for one word." He shook his head. "'Tis all gone. Youth and vigor have faded. Yob-Haggoth did not include immortality in the bargain. I still have one or two rhymes left in me, though. Or so I thought until I was captured. Perhaps there could be one about you, barbarian. From the sound of your voice, you're a vigorous fellow, with a courageous turn of mind. That, incidentally, will not serve you well in the world. Deceit is the order of—but I speak as though tomorrow existed for both of us." He lifted his blind head to the darkness where the bloated spiderlike thing stirred. "There is nothing for any of us now but the ritual. And death."

A dreadful silence fell.

Brak glanced at the blind minstrel again, then at the little bald Nestorian Friar who sat on the fire-pit coping, head bowed, mumbling over the stone cross that he cupped in his hands. Presently Tyresias stumbled a few paces off and started to hum a tune, raggedly and off key. The sound was jarring to the ear.

Brak began to circle the paving stones around the fire pit. He strode in an ever-widening circle, running his eyes over the walls. He found no crevice, no clue as to how to avoid the awful fate. In his heart coldness gathered. He started when a bell chimed low four times.

Tyresias sighed and ceased his humming. "'The false morn will soon be breaking outside. Then it won't be much more than one more inversion of the hourglass before full sunrise."

"We cannot just stand here like bull oxen waiting to be poled down!" Brak shouted.

The hoarseness of his cry set up odd wavering echoes in the chamber. Over them, blending with them, Brak heard another sound—brittle and piercing feminine laughter.

It was far away, tantalizing, tinkly as water over brook pebbles. Suddenly the air all around swam and dimmed.

Friar Jerome leaped to his feet. He held his cross out before him at arm's length. There was a dazzling pulse of white light, bursting, flaring, as though something alien had reacted angrily to that stone symbol. With a weak cry, Jerome tumbled to the stones, unconscious.

The cross had flown from his out-flung hand as he fell. With a peculiar dread he could not understand (the cryptic symbol meant nothing to him) Brak peered and saw that the cross lay a few paces from Jerome's fingers. It was shattered.

Tyresias began to quake. "She is here. She comes. *She comes again.*"

Twisting round, Brak saw the source of the light-blaze. The opalescent bubble was descending from the high darkness.

The bubble was still ebony at its rim, paler in its center. But now within it no dreamy-face watched. This time there was only a mist roiling with a sinister life.

The bubble dropped and dropped. Brak realized that it was descending swiftly, as if by plan, directly upon him.

Tyresias' shoulders shook violently. He sensed the peril. "Hell's Daughter visits again, outlander. It is not me she seeks, nor the Friar. Run! Run to the corner!"

A tightness in his throat, Brak nevertheless stood his ground. The dreadful specter of the bubble terrified him as it loomed over him with its center full of those awful, ceaselessly shifting mists. But he had decided that whatever would serve to take him from this chamber to another place where he might have the chance to use his wits and his fists, and perhaps even clutch a broadsword again, was good.

Confronting anything that gave him that dim chance would indeed be little worse than languishing here with an ineffectual priest and a burned-out singer of songs. So he struggled to control his fear. He dug his fingers into his own thighs to sting himself awake as the perimeter of the bubble danced radiantly before him and touched...

A thousand freezing nights on the high steppes, the wild lands of the north, could not have contained more bone-hurting cold than that bubble-skin that brushed against him. His heart slugged more slowly.

His vision dimmed. The roiling mists closed round his eyes and swallowed him.

Brak felt himself totally weightless then. He felt himself *rising upward*.

Finally he could see again. Below, he saw Friar Jerome fall away. The holy man still lay unconscious near his shattered cross. Tyresias hunched at the fire pit, shaking his head in pity. Brak was caught *within* the bubble now, prisoned there...

He flung out his arms, hands fisted. He flailed and struck at the freezing smoke which had a deliciously pleasant tang, despite the pain it brought to his naked hide. The more he struggled, the more he floundered in his curious weightless state. The bubble drifted slowly higher through the chamber.

Then the mists began to swirl more furiously. They darkened as the bubble neared the filthy webbing strung by the creature at the top of the vast hall. Oddly, strands of this webbing seemed to penetrate the bubble. Nauseated, Brak battled at them. He touched only freezing air.

The webbing had passed *through* the bubble, and *through* him, and now the bubble floated on upward again, touching the great stone-roofed vault and being absorbed *into it and through it*.

Brak glanced downward. With mortal fear, he saw his lower limbs dissolving, melting, *fading into and through the solid ceiling-blocks*. A strange numbness swept his body. It drove out the cold, as more and more of the bubble, more and more of his own mighty frame was absorbed. He was sinking *upward* through the wall. The line of the wall's surface crept up his belly—up the brawny planes of his chest, up his throat, across his chin. As his face sank upward into that numbing darkness, the last thing he heard was a tinkling, delighted laugh.

"Come, come, strong one," the gentle voice seemed to soothe. "Ariane is not so fearsome."

Knowing he was magically summoned, Brak cried out, "They called you Hell's Daughter. I want no part of you or...

Darkness slipped across his face and his mind as well.

Wind lashed his face. All about him Brak felt the thrust of it, buffeting him from one direction, than another. In the instant when this holocaust of keening sound first beat upon his mind, fear spurted fresh inside him, like the gush of some poisoned fountain. He fought for one terrible, careening moment to suppress the fear, but to no avail.

The wind flayed his face. It forced him to flick his eyes open. A league below, or so it seemed, the world tilted and slid away beneath the small, fragile car of moon-drenched copper in which he lurched back and forth. His belly flopped over with vertigo. He shot his hands out to catch the car's rail and steady himself. A sense of bedazzlement spread around and above and beneath him.

Brak the barbarian found himself riding in the ornamented copper car of a chariot that flew through the heavens. On the horizon the moon swam misty and full, a dazzling coin of light. In the east, far past the glinting blue frontiers of the Ice-marches, yonder toward the Mountains of Smoke where the goatherd Nestoriamus had died, pallid light crept to illumine the day.

Brak's heart pounded with terror. His body felt perilously light, both real and unreal, as though the self that rode up here above the world, rode here upon the wind in this chariot with a beautiful weirdling holding the reins, was not his real self but merely some wizard's projection. His barbarian's mind struggled to encompass within the space of a few seconds all the wonders he could view from the awful vantage point.

Along the near southwestern horizon, the city of Kambda Kai crouched in darkness. Nearer, looming up from the ice-crusted blue rocks, rose an immense stone carving, tall and huge around. The chariot was sweeping through the sky away from it. Gradually the strange monolith took on definition.

It was a mammoth ruined idol, the squatting figure of a semi-human thing with brutal stone fists resting upon its crossed thighs and its sinister mouth turned downward, as though to curse all of the land that its fearsome stone eyes surveyed. Suddenly Brak realized that this mighty idol in the wilderness must be the image of Yob-Haggoth.

Of more immediate concern to him was the girl who held the reins of the chariot in her chalk-white hands. She turned her head, glancing at him over her shoulder while her ebony hair streamed behind her. It twisted and tangled with the misty-black robe she wore, so that it was impossible to tell exactly where hair and gown intermingled.

Ariane's lips were curled into a curious, speculative smile. Her little teeth were bared to the wind and her eyes were wide as she worked to control the reins.

Out in front of those gossamer-gray strands, a pair of strange horse-like creatures with silver bits in their jaws lunged ahead through empty sky, great black hides rippling. Never had Brak seen such monsters, even in his most fevered dreams. The incredible stallions had manes that *burned*. Banners of fire trailed from their distended nostrils, shooting iridescent scarlet and orange and yellow sparks back into the night.

"Why have you brought me here, woman?" Brak bawled above the wind's tumult.

"Do you really know who I am, barbarian?" the girl laughed back. "Have they told you, those two dung heaps whose time has all run out?"

"You're the woman who gulled me in Kambda Kai. A strumpet enchantress."

This angered Ariane. She whipped round and flicked the end of one of the gossamer reins against his cheek. The rein cut a wicked runnel thin as a knife's edge down Brak's cheek.

He reached up to swab at the blood. His fingers came away dry. The wound had already closed over, though its pain still stung.

Now at last Brak was certain that neither he nor Ariane were real. His body (his corpse, perhaps?) slumbered down there in the shrine of Yob-Haggoth while his damned soul rode up here with this black-eyed witch girl and the fire-maned horses drew the copper car downward across the sky.

The girl said through clenched teeth, "I am Ariane, the daughter of Septegundus. I command respect."

"Since when must a man respect foulness?" Brak called back.

At once a subtle change came into Ariane's eyes. She tugged lightly at the reins again. With incredible slowness and grace, yet with a speed testified to by the roaring wind, the fire-maned horses turned in the sky and sped southward. Ariane said: "The Darter boys told me you were just a peasant clod out of the north. Yet you seem capable of fairly subtle turns of mind, Brak."

"You know my name."

"Aye. And more."

"Well, I know yours, too. And more important, the meaning of it."

She whispered it, making it sound both mocking, and like a tempting sweetmeat: "Ariane, Ariane. *Ariane.*"

"Daughter of Hell is what the Friar said."

Ariane shrugged. The diaphanous blackness of her gown gave a sudden wild flutter, blowing over her and wrapping itself around Brak's neck.

The fabric caressed his cheek with a subtle, sensuously perfumed pressure. He tore the black stuff away. The wind whipped it back toward Ariane, whose white cheeks gleamed in the glare of the fire streaming from the manes of the phantom horses.

The moon had nearly set. The Ice-marches had vanished back into the blue haze at the world's north rim. Ahead, a golden city spread on a plain.

"The Friar's tongue will clack more softly when Yob-Haggoth gathers him in, Brak. He has put poison in your mind about me."

This almost made Brak throw his head back and bray with savage laughter. "Poison! Gods, woman, what more would be needed than a clubbing and an enchantment followed by imprisonment and the knowledge that I'm to be part of some sacrifice to appease a filthy power of whom I have never heard?"

Now black sparks glittered in Ariane's eyes. Lightly she flicked the reins, to show him that she could sting him again.

"Do not blaspheme. Yob-Haggoth is the Dark One. The Supreme One." "What of it? What do you want of me? You watched me from that enchanted bubble when I was first inside the idol. For what reason?"

A little pink tongue crawled over Ariane's lips as she moistened them. Then she countered, "What else did the wicked Nestorian tell you about me? That I take lovers? Well, that is so. My father and I are not wholly creatures of the world. But still, we share certain earthly hungers which come with these bodies we inhabit. You are a man of parts, barbarian. Strong. Equipped with a certain primitive courage. Courage, I might say, would be of very little value to you in the world. Such virtues are not prized among men. If you were a small man, a trickster, free of scruples—ah, then, barbarian, then you might reach Khurdisan."

Brak turned cold again. She knew of his quest and dream. But he kept silent as she went on: "Aye, then you might reach Khurdisan alive. But the world does not want your kind. Nor will the world do anything but punish a man like you who rides by his own lights, defiantly." She laughed again. "It is our world, my father's and mine. A black, tormented pit of a place."

Brak's thick yellow brows quirked together. "How is it you know I was bound for Khurdisan?"

"I know everything about you. I have sucked your mind dry like an apricot seed. It is a simple mind in many ways. Not so simple in others." The teasing, lustful smile returned. "All in all, I find you of considerable attraction."

"You're mocking me with all this talk, woman. I am fated to die. Already the light breaks."

Ariane waved one long-nailed hand as the great gilt city with its domes and cupolas, its immense market squares and temples, glided by beneath them. They swept down the world, swift as the wind that bore them.

"The ritual is of no consequence, Brak."

"Of no consequence!"

"No, because I can alter the outcome."

"Save my life?"

"Yes. The Darter boys can find another unbeliever in the stews of Kambda Kai in time."

His belly hardened, deathly cold in the center. A strange crisis, one which he was ill equipped to comprehend or deal with. The crisis was upon him.

"For this there would be a price, eh, woman?"

Ariane leaned toward him. Sparks from the blazing horses' manes caught in her hair, shone like jewels of fire.

"Yes, barbarian. Yes, a price. You bind yourself to me."

"For how long? Until Hell cracks open and the world bows to Yob-Haggoth?"

A wild light shone in her eyes. "That time will not be long in coming, Brak, mark me. How long there remains an—interest—between us is my right to say. Mine alone. But you would have to grant me that right freely, for that right is one thing I cannot take from you by a spell. Your alternative is simply the completion of the sacrificial rite."

With one fierce, sweeping turn, Brak faced away from her and confronted the encompassing horizon, the gilt city dropping behind, a dun-colored plain sweeping up ahead.

Upon the plain an army maneuvered in the dawn light. Brak saw tens upon tens of thousands of horse and footmen, and scythe chariots, and heralds blowing great bronze war horns of teardrop shape. He saw a panoply of martial splendors such as he had merely imagined in his youth.

The dream chariot raced above the sea of aquamarine and yellow and emerald and royal purple pennons which dipped and whipped on lance tips. And none in the great host saw the phantom chariot overhead.

Brak made a savage gesture that took in all this richness of armed might. "Why do you ask the question here, Ariane? Why *here*, woman? Why here, where I can see all this? Why do you ask in this car which almost flies faster than the light itself, over wonders I've never seen before?"

Ariane did not answer directly. Her mouth gleamed softly as she lifted it toward him. "Let me have your soul, barbarian."

"I know nothing of words like that. I am sure I have a thick right arm to wield a sword, and two limbs to carry me, but as for other things..."

"You have a soul," she whispered. "'But you must grant it freely."

"As the minstrel Tyresias granted it?"

"What?"

"With the skewering of his eyes by your own hand?"

Ariane seemed caught up in some sensual trance. She did no react to the words with anger as he expected, only seemed to relax and sway gently against his bronzed forearm. Her cheek touched his skin with an odd softness that aroused thick, evil thoughts in his mind.

He fought the thoughts as she rubbed her cheek against his forearm and murmured, "Brak, Brak, my strong one. There is nothing, nothing in the great world which does not have a price that must be paid for it. I can offer you so much. My own love, and more. All you want of the world and its jeweled cities. If you do not believe how wonderful it is—*look!*"

The last word was a jubilant cry as she whipped the reins down upon the backs of the horses.

The wind increased. In moments the copper car was traveling with a swiftness that made Brak clutch its rail and fear for his life.

Beneath him streamed the kingdoms of the world resplendent in the dawn. He saw great border walls and turquoise seas where fat merchantmen plowed under bright-colored sail. Strange shrines and forgotten cities loomed in yellow deserts, and there were craggy mountain regions, and silver mines chopped from the peaks where thousands upon thousands of men labored, antlike, to gather the raw gleaming silver stuff.

Onward the chariot sped down the sky, past castles, forests, glades, prairies, uplands, over battling armies and tribes of desert nomads wandering, past lofty enamelled city spires where holy men cried into the sunrise, on and on and on in a mad, dazzling pattern of sights and splendors of such hurting beauty as to nearly crack a man's mind.

Under the plowing hoofs of the chariot that raced between land and stars, all the kingdoms of the world fled by as she cried their magic names aloud—Phrixos and Phryx and Toct, Gat and Chambalor and Ringarim, Bemkah and Kopt, Tyros and Thanzid and Tobool.

And then, burning with a yellow haze in a great encompassing crescent at the south edge of the world, there it was. Brak's heart quickened fearsomely. Above the wind Ariane lashed the horses maniacally and shrieked: "Khurdisan, Brak my beloved. *Khurdisan the Golden.*"

White knuckled, he clutched the rail, straining for a glimpse of it behind the shining golden mist upon the horizon.

Suddenly Ariane's laughter bubbled up and died. With a sharp, "Hai! *Hai!*" she lashed the horses again and jerked the reins. The chariot swung round the sky, into the north.

The gilt glow of Khurdisan fled behind them. Ariane murmured, "Not yet, Brak. Ah, not yet. That will only be yours if you bind yourself and give yourself freely to me."

Temptation enflamed him. Doubt and guilt assailed him. What would be so wrong in it, one awful part of his mind argued. Was she not comely, exceedingly fair? Would not her arms be warm and perfumed? She would spare his life! And he could bargain! He could be in golden Khurdisan in a twinkling, just as soon as she tired of him. He opened his lips to speak a yes, for it would be so easy.

Ariane's black-velvet eyes glowed in anticipation. She leaned toward him eagerly. Into Brak's mind flashed the hideous image of Tyresias and his sewn-shut eyes. There was evil in the world. That much of Jerome's prating he believed. *This* was evil.

"No," he grumbled, his whole body hurting from the effort required to say that single word. Then again, with a roar, "No! No!" He beat his huge fists on the car rail. His savage yellow braid trailed out behind him in the wind as he bawled, "No, hell-woman! That part of me you will not have! I cannot believe I have a soul, but the shine in your eyes tells me I must. And I say *no*!"

For a moment Ariane's face wrenched in hate. Then her eyes narrowed, intensely curious. She studied the agonized posture of the barbarian as he hung on the car rail, head tossed back, teeth bared, eyes shut. He prayed to nameless gods whose origins and powers he did not know, praying for strength to resist this temptation.

And Ariane saw that he was strong, and somehow this produced not fury, but a sadness.

From around her neck she slipped a small silver chain with a bauble hanging on it. Before Brak could stop her, she had looped this chain over his head. The bauble's gentle pressure on his chest brought his eyes open.

The thing made his flesh tingle where it touched. He saw that it was a tiny replica of that weird bubble in which she had descended, a black-rimmed jewel with a heart of whirling gray stuff.

Ariane touched his cheek. "My poor barbarian. I should hate you with all my being. I do not. I want you still."

He shook his head, turned away. He did not want to look into her beautiful eyes too long. All around, clouds whirled now, black streamers of them obscuring the world, as though the dawn through which the chariot had raced were an illusion. The fire-maned horses were descending. Brak could tell by the tilt of the car. Like a sad theme of music, the memory of golden Khurdisan shining on the horizon reappeared in his mind. Was it forever lost?

"With the little bubble," Ariane said, "I chain myself to you. I bind myself to you, even unto the moment of your death. Until that moment you can change your mind, barbarian. You can call me with the bubble. Touch it and whisper my name. I will come. Otherwise…" Her face hardened. "Yob-Haggoth is the Supreme One. Yob-Haggoth will be served."

"Damn Yob-Haggoth and this world I do not understand!" he cried, but the words were blown away by a sudden clap of thunder that boomed through the black fog. The car, Ariane, the dreamsteeds, all disintegrated.

He flailed his arms for balance. His vision darkened. He was afraid. He very nearly reached up to touch the glassy bubble hanging on his chest. He fought against the desire.

In the whirling dark he heard vile, jolly laughter. It was the laughter of Septegundus, welcoming him. *Blackness.*

Blackness thick and billowing. The maniacal laugh rose and rose in a malicious crescendo. Like throbbing drums, the laughter burst against Brak's ears while the foul black smoke blew and whipped all around him. He thrust his palms against his ears. Still the noise persisted, making his temples beat with hurt. Louder than thunder. Louder than a hundred-thousand warriors moving together across the earth.

In a burst of blue light, all the smoky chaos burned up, blinded him, vanished. He felt himself falling. He plummeted through nothing, sightless. His throat clogged with terror. In one more flick of an eyelid the spell was broken, and the final horror loomed.

Thin bluish sunlight reflecting from the icy sweeps of the cold-rimed land pulsed and hurt his eyes.

Directly over Brak's head a fearsome stone image leered down.

His mind cleared slowly. He recognized the mammoth ruined idol, frozen for all time in green-shot granite. Its body seemed to exude a foul dampness even though the dawn air was dry and frosty.

The closed stone fists of Yob-Haggoth rested upon the crossed stone thighs just above Brak, and the higher portions of the image seemed to shoot into the pale morning heavens. The huge chiseled eyes regarded the world implacably. The stone mouth curved downward in a cruel grimace.

Brak heard stirrings to either side. He was sprawled on his back. There was cold stone beneath him. He turned his head to the right.

Tyresias lay there, eyes turned up to a sky he could not see. On Brak's left, Friar Jerome was rousing, sitting halfway up now, shaking his bald head. Brak discovered that the three of them were lying on an immense stone platform that jutted out from the idol's base.

As Brak propped himself up on one hand, he wondered how he and the other two had gotten out here into the pale light of dawn. Then he realized that they must have been carried. Behind him he heard shuffling footsteps.

Twisting round, he saw a double line of the Darter boys emerge from a portal obscured with shadows. This doorway was set into one of Yob-Haggoth's knees.

Scrambling up, Brak glanced both left and right again. His face wrenched with savage fury. They were hemmed in.

The Darter boys, two score now, then three, swiftly ranged themselves around the rim of the rectangular platform. They faced inward, toward the trio of sacrifices.

The Nestorian said, "You slept deeply, barbarian. Ariane took your mind away for a time and left your body. You whimpered and moaned and thrashed around on the floor of the prison hall. Once you climbed up on your knees as though you wanted to throw yourself over the coping into the fire pit. I had to drag you back. Your eyes remained tightly shut the whole time. After a while you seemed to lose the fury. As though she had released you. I grew drowsy then. I remember nothing else until we wakened here a moment ago."

Scowling and squinting, Brak watched the Darter boys range themselves round the platform's edge. Their eyes shone. Their silver-needle fingers clicked at their sides, *click-clack-click-clack*. The faint sound made an ominous counterpoint to the wind's keen.

Yob-Haggoth's image leered out at the world. From the doorway which led inside the shrine, there were rustlings and stirrings.

Tyresias clutched the Friar's arm, shaking like a reed in rain. "Holy Friar, call on your Nameless God. Beg him to save usl"

Wearily Jerome shook his head. "I do not command Him. Nor does He answer like a lackey. Those who swear faith to Him still remain men, beset by a man's perils. My only power, the stone cross, is smashed. I..."

Jerome started. He had noticed the thin silver chain hanging around Brak's neck. His mouth soured. "What is that you wear, barbarian? Her mark?"

The Friar made as if to grab the bauble and tear it off. Brak seized the Nestorian's wrist. He closed his fingers on flesh and bone until Jerome winced.

Through peeled-back lips Brak said, "To touch it will summon her. If that happens, she'll fetch me for her own."

Tyresias nodded his head feebly. "What price did she offer to pay, outlander?"

For a moment Brak's heart was near to breaking. "The world. And Khurdisan of the south."

Somehow Jerome managed a bit of wryness: "Well, old singer, the price quoted appears to be higher than simply a set of powerful lungs and a molten voice. Perhaps it's because our barbarian friend is young."

"I'll have none of her!" Brak began. Suddenly his spine crawled. He felt someone watching, someone other than the Darter boys. He snapped his head up.

There, above him, standing in the frosted wind of the pale early morning, barefoot, with her ebony silks whipping around her and mingling with her hair, was Ariane. She watched from a perch atop Yob-Haggoth's immense right knee. She lifted one hand as though to beckon.

How easy it would be, Brak thought with weariness. How easy to touch the bauble. Call her name. Surrender and be done with this quiet, evil place. In the cold wastes of black rock and blue, frozen pools, Yob-Haggoth towered thirty times higher than a man. At his feet the Darter boys clicked their needle-fingers in soft, anticipatory rhythm, *click-clack-click-clack*.

Brak's gorge rose. Was he a puling child to be frightened into docility? The hot reeking blood of wolves ran in his body. He would not whimper or cower. He would die as befitted a man of the wild lands of the north. He'd take some of these crawling vermin along to the unknown Pit, too.

What he needed was a weapon. A weapon, so that he could die with his head upraised, chanting his rage.

The *click-clack-click-clack* of fingers intensified. Out from the portal of the shrine marched a square formation of Darter boys, three to a side. In the center another of the ragged wretches carried a polished sheet of metal upon which rested five objects. A scrap of robe which Brak quickly decided matched the color of Tyresias' ragged garments and must have been ripped from them; the two stone fragments of the broken cross; and Brak's own broadsword.

"So that is where the cross went," Friar Jerome whispered. "Evidently they need some token from each of us to complete the ritual."

"Huh," Brak hissed back. "If I can but lay my hands on that blade…"

"There will be no time," Jerome answered. "Mark well the fifth object on the tray."

This Brak did. His belly chilled again. Lying beside the other items was a short, thick dagger of bronze. Its blade was green with tarnish, except for certain places where the bronze was totally obscured by a black coating of old, dried blood. The knobbed hilt of the ceremonial knife was shaped into a head of Yob-Haggoth.

The square formation approached within a half-dozen paces of the three victims. Then the Darter boys halted, and stepped to the side, leaving the keeper of the tray holding his burden in proud, blind-eyed isolation.

Desperately Brak swept the scene again. The rocks and tundras were empty of all other sign of human beings. Perhaps this place was so accursed that no travelers ever ventured near. And he searched in vain for some other portal leading back into the idol. The door onto the platform seemed to be the only one.

One final time Brak looked up at the figure of the stone god. He noticed a large fissure about half way up the idol's belly. But the fissure would not serve as a hiding place, or a place to wedge in, turn and fight. It was barely half a hand's width at its widest.

One of the Darter boys flung his head back and howled, "*The bringer of Yob-Haggoth!* The bringer of Yob-Haggoth!" Every other Darter boy took up the cry: "The bringer of Yob-Haggoth comes! The bringer of Yob-Haggoth comes! *Septegundus comes! SEPTEGUNDUS COMES!*"

And from the black portal silently glided the Amyr of Evil upon Earth.

Brak jammed his knuckles into his eye sockets in disbelief. The man was not of overwhelming stature. He was clad in a plain black robe with voluminous sleeves into which his hands were folded. His pate was closely shaven, his nose aquiline, his lips thin. His chin formed a sharp point, and the upper parts of his ears were pointed, too.

His eyes were large, dark, staring, nearly all pupil. Very little white showed. He had no eyelids. Evidently they had been removed by a crude surgical procedure. Light pads of scar tissue had encrusted above the sockets which held eyes that never closed.

But what turned Brak's belly to a lumpy mass of terror was Septegundus' very flesh. It was *alive*. It *crawled*. The skin was etched on every inch of its surface with human figures. Tiny, naked human figures, hundreds of them, intertwined and slowly writhing in postures of eternal torment. The figures were somehow prisoned *within* the thin layers of flesh and were crawling slowly there, crawling, *moving*, in a never-ending pattern variation of bodies, arms, legs, torsos.

Brak wanted to bite down on his lip until blood ran.

Ceremoniously Septegundus glided forward until he stood directly before them. "Welcome three," he said in a light, reedy voice. He bowed to Tyresias. "Welcome, believer. We have met before." A bow to Friar Jerome. "Welcome, priest." And then he bent at the waist and fixed those dreadful whiteless eyes upon Brak, who stood rigid and sweating at the incredible spectacle of human misery crawling and turning upon the forehead of Septegundus.

"Welcome, unbeliever," Septegundus said. "You did not choose the way my daughter offered you, so the thrice-fired hells of Yob-Haggoth shall be yours."

As though mesmerized, Brak could not rip his own gaze from that of Septegundus. The creature (how could he be thought of as a man?) cracked a merciless smile.

"Still, there is time left, barbarian. I wish only pleasure for my child. We can yet find another to take your place so that Yob-Haggoth may drink the warm blood and be renewed in his power. My child is a beautiful child. She could offer you the most tempting of delights, the most…"

In that moment, as the voice of Septegundus prattled on, somehow feeble despite the palpable aura of evil power that radiated around him, Brak's last thin veneer of civility and sense cracked away. With one awful, animal yell he gathered spittle in his mouth, blew it in the crawling face of Septegundus and gave the foul creature a mighty buffet with his balled right hand.

Tyresias arched his back as though he had been lanced with exquisite pain when he heard Septegundus cry out. "Fool, oh you fool!" Tyresias shrieked. Septegundus tumbled backwards, flapping his hands free of his robes. The flesh of those hands crawled and crawled with tiny, tormented human figures, too.

Brak leaped. He laid hands upon Septegundus and flung him back against the Darter boy with the salver. Instantly black night descended, blotting out the landscape. Red lightning cracked in the heart of this sudden blackness and struck the stone platform and burned and hissed.

There was a thunderclap. Another. The red lightnings danced and flickered again, blasting to the right of Brak, then to the left. The platform heated beneath his naked soles, blistering hot. Smoke poured in from all directions. The eyes of the Darter boys flamed with reflections of the red lightnings as they rushed forward.

Blackness filled the world. Brak leaped forward with another howl. The stone image of Yob-Haggoth towered. Red lightnings played around it, sparking. Septegundus had recovered himself, was thrashing in the smoke and crying wild, meaningless incantations.

Brak stumbled against the Darter boy with the salver. He closed his hands around the magical boy's throat. The salver fell. Brak wrenched the Darter boy to the left, snapping his neck with one constriction of his fingers.

Then Brak bent down and scrabbled in the smoke. All around thunder pounded and the red lightnings crisscrossed, sizzling past the barbarian with the smell of perdition in them. Brak could not find the hilt of his fallen sword.

His fingers ached as he quested down into the whirling smoke. Somewhere Tyresias bleated in terror. Somewhere Friar Jerome mumbled a dimly heard prayer. At last Brak's hurting fingers touched something cold, hard, and familiar. He closed his fingers and jerked upward. The red lightnings blazed and glared on the blade of the broadsword he had retrieved.

Septegundus tottered at him through the billowing smoke, hands upraised. In each hand was a writhing, wet-scaled black serpent with a triple-forked tongue, a serpent long as Brak was tall. Septegundus gave a thin, derisive cry and hurled first one serpent, then the other.

With a mighty hack of the blade, Brak sliced one of the foul beasts in half. Its parts twitched away to be lost in the smoke. The other snake slithered past his shoulder and the triple-forked tongue darted out to the nearest target, the neck of a Darter boy charging in to fight.

One kiss of that tongue and the Darter boy reeled back, eyes bulging. He shook with a fatal ague while the serpent wrapped its coils round and round his neck.

Brak fought. He drove his sword left, through a Darter boy's throat. He pulled it out, slammed it to the right and lopped off another head. It spun away, fountaining blood from the neck. Thunder roared incessantly. Brak's brain was full of fear and madness, for his savage attack upon Septegundus had somehow unleashed the power of Yob-Haggoth.

Up there in the blowing blackness the image of Yob-Haggoth was beginning to shudder and vibrate. Its surface was played over by the glare of the red lightnings. One bolt struck the idol's head. Another hit its belly. Each time the stone grew more luminous, until the entire idol was pulsing an eerie scarlet. Its stone eyes burned brightest of all.

Somewhere off in the murk Septegundus mouthed spells noisily. A rain of lizards and toads fell all around Brak. He trampled and smashed them underfoot. A hand plucked at his elbow. He whirled, ready to hack off the head of another Darter boy. The hand slipped off. The smoke was so thick that Septegundus' acolytes were confused. They bumped against one another. Their curses added to the din.

The sweating face of Friar Jerome appeared. His mouth worked violently, panting: "You have roused Yob-Haggoth himself. Look." Jerome pointed up.

Scarlet light seemed to shine from within the very stone of the idol now. The stone eyes flamed. Brilliant red beams shone out from the fissure in the idol's belly. It was as though a foul living essence of evil had gathered within the image and was pouring forth.

"Yob-Haggoth *come*!" Septegundus shrieked, his face looming briefly in the murk. "*Yob-Haggoth send down thy power and aid thy servant!*"

In dreadful fascination, Brak peered high upward at the light seeping out through the fissure in the idol's belly. It was the light of evil seeping out, seeping out through an opening which—

An *opening*? With a wild yell, broadsword raised, Brak ran. Darter boys like half-real phantasms blocked his charge through the billowing murk. Brak swung his broadsword left and right, left and right in murderous arcs, and slew them. Some primeval fear told him that the world was shattering, coming to an end in thunder and searing blasts of lightning that sent fierce red sparks burning and hissing against his skin. If this were so and all was doomed, he had nothing left to lose, so he let the wild fighting madness possess him.

There was no more civilized restraint left in him. He was the savage, seeking to wreak as much hell as he could, and his broadsword sang back and forth like a gory scythe.

A few spurts of fire sizzled toward him from the fingertips of the Darter boys. Brak managed to dodge past these and soon none of the acolytes attacked any longer, for his broad-sword had proved a fierce weapon. It hung in his slack right hand as he blundered blindly into the carved and crossed stone legs of Yob-Haggoth. From Brak's blade rivulets of red dripped. Bits of human brain and cartilage clung to the cutting edge. His entire body was smeared with this scarlet and gray dabbing. As he struggled to jump high and catch the upper horizontal edge of the crossed leg, a still-wet human handprint, marked in blood, glistened out on the naked flesh of his back where his long yellow braid swayed.

With one hand Brak seized the stone leg's upper edge. He flung the broadsword up and over so that he might use both hands to pull himself upward. This he did with considerable effort, conscious of how the night's ordeal had drained his strength. Hate was in his balefully glinting eyes as he dragged himself forward across the stone to where the sword lay. His all-encompassing desire for revenge buoyed him a little, gave him the strength to seize the sword and stagger forward to do what he must.

The holocaust of smoke, lightning, and thunder increased. It was almost beyond human bearing, a wild, phantasmagoric interplay of fights and noise. Down below on the platform, Septegundus was howling to Yob-Haggoth for succor. Above Brak the evil idol pulsed with its sinister glow, and this awful brilliance fit its eyes and continued to pour out through the fissure in its belly.

Suddenly another magical rain descended upon the lurching barbarian. There were spiders by the hundreds. Some were fat and yellow and oozing transparent liquid poisons through the tips of their feelers, others were small, quick, and mottled. Shuddering, Brak tore three, six, then whole handfuls of them from his arms and torso and stamped others under his feet, staggering ahead through the awful putrefying ruin of their squashed bodies.

He slammed against the idol's stone belly, recoiled with a cry. The stone was simmering, weirdly flaccid. It had lost its solidity and become a scalding, undulating tissue of evil that lived, lived, and poured hot hell glare out through the fissure just above Brak's head.

A delirium was beginning to fill his mind. It seemed that the monstrous stone head of Yob-Haggoth began to incline downward then, turn downward upon its stone neck.

Not possible! his mind cried out, fighting off the fear the terrible illusion created. And yet he knew somehow that it was possible, with Septegundus calling upon all the necromantic force of his evil god-master.

The area in which Brak stood balanced perilously on the idol's crossed legs began to brighten to an unbearable radiance. The light poured from Yob-Haggoth's eyes and boiled smoking out of the split stone.

Then the god looked down.

In but a few more heartbeats, Brak felt, he would die. He cursed the unknown gods that had drawn him to this inglorious fate. He fastened his hands on the hilt of his broadsword. He brought the broadsword up over his head with one last burst of effort, fingers locked atop the hilt, palm-butts supporting the hilt from underneath as though it were a double-handed spear. And with every mighty thew and every great muscle in his body wrenching and writhing, he gave a frenzied scream of hate and drove the sword into the fissure of light.

Winds of monumental force tore at him, threatening to blow him from his perch. The billowing smoke became even darker. A smell of the tomb, a stink of ten-thousand corpses rotting fumed within a palpable cloud that gushed from the fissure.

The light within the idol began to dim. The thunderclaps blended one into another without interruption. Brak's own vision grew feeble as he tottered in the screaming wind.

The world was darkening. The statue of Yob-Haggoth was changing from living, undulating light back to sickly green-shot stone. From within the statue's heart came a titanic grinding.

"You barbarian *filth*!"

Brak twisted around, gasping in horror. Crawling up over the edge of the crossed stone legs came Septegundus, the repulsive images on his flesh still turning, writhing, twisting. His lidless eyes stood out in that crawling face like inhuman dark lanterns. In his right hand Septegundus clutched the bronze dagger with the head of Yob-Haggoth fashioned into its hilt.

Brak felt his legs grow weak and wavery. He tried to brace himself against the hardening, cooling stone of the rumbling idol. With his face radiating ultimate evil, Septegundus clambered to his feet and fixed Brak with his pitiless stare. Then he released the bronze dagger.

Incredibly, the dagger hung suspended, shaking faintly in the air that roiled between them. Septegundus' supple, image-etched hands whipped back and forth in strange, mystic gestures. His lips, blood-blackened where he had bit them through in rage, formed syllables Brak did not understand.

The barbarian knew he must move, dodge, flee, try to escape. But the wind battered him, and his senses no longer served him well. His right leg shook with a violent muscle spasm. It buckled.

The dagger floating before Septegundus began to glow cherry colored. Slow and straight, it sailed forward through the air toward Brak's huge, panting chest.

For one cataclysmic moment the scene held: the bloodstained barbarian sunk to one knee, staring dully; the servant of Yob-Haggoth suddenly throwing his arm above his head, forming fists and howling in glee; and between them the slowly-rotating blade piercing the air straight and true for Brak's breastbone.

Brak had no strength, no energy, no wits left to move or avoid it. Onward the dagger flew, looming in his vision. And then, as if by instinct, his right hand clawed up to his throat. He clutched the bauble on the silver chain. He cried through the tumult: *"Ariane!"*

There was quicksilver blur. She materialized facing him, triumph in her eyes. Ariane bent forward to suck out his soul with a gentle kiss of her plum lips on his. Her fingers touched his gore-stained shoulders. Her hair blew all around like a wild black web as she brought her face nearer, ever nearer, whispering sweet foul words to him.

"Daughter!" Septegundus cried, but it was too late. Ariane's fingertips made claws on Brak's shoulder. Her fingers dug and ripped flesh away as her back arched violently. Her eyes locked with Brak's and comprehension of her pain blazed out. Then the lovely eyes glazed.

With one last yell, Brak dragged himself away. He leaped far out into the swirling, empty smokiness beyond the grinding, swaying idol. As he fell he saw Ariane likewise fall, her father's dagger implanted in her back, still rotating slowly to burrow itself ever deeper in her flesh.

Septegundus knelt over her. Above him, a mammoth crack appeared in the top of Yob-Haggoth's stone skull. The crack worked its way downward swiftly, splitting the image in half.

Septegundus snatched up his daughter in his arms. He pulled her against the bosom of his robe. He turned his head outward, toward Brak who was falling as though suspended in a dream. The eyes of the sorcerer caught Brak's and held for one knock of time, promising that Septegundus would find revenge.

Suddenly Brak's body struck stone jarringly, rolled. He had hit a portion of the lower platform. Smoke darkened his vision. Great chunks of Yob-Haggoth's image began to shear away and tumble as the red lightnings burst in a new frenzy.

Brak's pain increased, drove out the sight of Septegundus as Yob-Haggoth toppled.

Brak went rolling on, downward over rough stones. Through the cataclysm of sound he heard the voice of the sorcerer whispering, somehow sharp and clear and close. It brought to Brak a mortal dread: "The road is long to Khurdisan, barbarian. *I will be there.*"

Down Brak slammed, rolling and rolling over rocks he could not see. The awful promise echoed in his brain... *I will be there. I WILL BE THERE. I WILL...*

A cool, piercing silence engulfed him. It rang in his ears like the echo of nothing, of a world empty and destroyed. There was no more.

Tyresias and Friar Jerome had lived.

They fled from the platform in the maelstrom following Brak's attack upon Septegundus. After Brak fell free of the collapsing idol, the two men dragged the burly barbarian to the shelter of some rimed boulders.

The Nestorian priest dressed the worst of Brak's wounds with unguents from a pouch at his waist. The sun stood straight overhead, fierce and blue-yellow when Brak woke. His entire body was a mass of torment. Unmoving, he rested.

Tyresias sat against a rock, his legs straight out. He mumbled an incoherent tune. Friar Jerome knelt through the long hours of afternoon, hands clasped, head bowed as he prayed to his Nameless God.

Finally at sunset, Brak had the strength to regain his feet and stagger toward the ruins. The tumbled-in, wrecked image of Yob-Haggoth now cast a long shadow on the cold plain of the Ice-marches. Feeling drained of emotion, Brak clambered up over the stones. They were piled in a tremendous mound, having collapsed upon themselves. Ghastly fragments of the dead bodies of Darter boys lay wedged between the shattered pieces of rock.

Here a cold, pocked gray stone eye of Yob-Haggoth watched the emerging stars in the orange-streaked heavens. There a shattered fist lay clenched but powerless. Rooting in the ruins and still half-delirious, Brak saw dull metal wink.

He gave a low growl. He reached down with one straining arm and caught up his broadsword. An omen? The cutting edge was nicked, but otherwise the weapon was unharmed.

Not wishing to think or remember, Brak climbed down from the tumbled ruins again and shuffled toward the rock where Friar Jerome was tending a small campfire built from shrub twigs he had laboriously gathered. Jerome was on his knees, blowing into the flames he had kindled with his flint. Brak lumbered into the flickering circle. His broadsword dangled from his right hand. He held it tight, as a child would clasp some childish talisman.

"Where are they?" Brak's voice was so hoarse he could barely speak. The chill night wind of the Ice-marches brushed against his skin, prickling it. The wind carried a sound like the clinking of caravan-bells perhaps half a league off. In a moment the sound was gone.

Friar Jerome's eyes were strained with the shadows of fatigue. "Septegundus?"

"Yes," said Brak.

"Gone."

"Dead?"

"Never dead. Away for a time. Retreated. Hidden in whatever foul universe created Yob-Haggoth. A separate world, I think. Unseen by us, but just an eyeblink away for those whose souls the Dark One takes. You killed only the images of Septegundus and his daughter, Brak. You can never kill them."

Forlornly Brak peered up at the stars, estimating direction. He swung round until he could scan the velvet darkness of the southern sky. Strange constellations winked white and beckoning.

"He said he would be there, somewhere along the road to Khurdisan," Brak whispered.

Friar Jerome nodded. "Then he will be, and the Daughter of Hell as well. No man has ever mocked them so bitterly as you did with that iron tooth."

Slowly Jerome rose. The fire was crackling now. Brushing his pudgy hands against his robe to dash off a few ashes, he approached the brooding barbarian whose eyes burned dully as he stared into the blaze.

Jerome laid a hand on Brak's shoulder. "Turn back. You would be wiser."

"There is nothing to which I can return, holy man. I will leave you and go south until I can steal or buy a pony. Then I will ride."

I will be there. The words rang faintly in Brak's brain, filling him with terror. *I will be there.* It was not an idle promise.

Friar Jerome pondered. "Very well, then. I travel the roads of this world too. Perhaps we shall encounter one another again. Come, I caught a hare while you slept. It's a poor emaciated thing, but Tyresias says his hands are steady enough to skin it. We can sup."

Starlight softened the ruins of the unspeakable shrine of Yob-Haggoth. Brak glanced at them and glanced away. He gave a short, sharp shake of his head.

"I want to be away from this place. Put it far behind me. I have had enough of the world for one night."

"And yet you're willing to go on," Jerome said.

Suddenly Brak's spirits seemed to lighten a little. He rubbed a sore place in his arm, kneaded it with his powerful fingers until some of the ache abated. Then he shrugged.

"Fate writes, holy man. Even this iron tooth as you call it cannot lop off that hand."

Jerome fumbled at his belt, producing a small cross of Nestoriamus which he had apparently fashioned of twigs tied together with a thin green strip of tundra-shrub bark.

"You do not belong in this world, barbarian. You belong in a simpler world where men do not deal dishonestly with one another, or traffic with devils. If you will not turn back to your homeland, take this to protect you."

Almost longingly Brak peered at the stick cross. Then again he shook his head.

"I am not a child of your god. I cannot."

"You are his child but you do not know it."

"Then if I am ignorant of the fact, 'tis the same thing." Impatiently now, for the conversation was beginning to puzzle and embarrass him, Brak hefted his broadsword and slapped it across his left shoulder, resting it there lightly while his hand curled around the hilt.

"I salute you, priest. I salute you, singer," he called across the firelight.

Veined old hands busy with a knife which he plied on the hare's skinny body, Tyresias did not hear. The minstrel seemed to be caught up in some sort of private vision. He hummed to himself. Miraculously, the old lips were turned up at the corners in a lonely smile.

Jerome said, "He is making a song, I think. He has been at it all day, ever since we realized we had lived thanks to your courage. I heard him sing your name several times. His voice sounded firmer and clearer than before. Perhaps one day as you travel you will hear someone sing the song he's making up about you." Jerome looked at him long and then added, "There is that kind of legend in you. And in your sword."

Shrugging again and shaking his head so that the long yellow braid settled in place behind him, Brak turned on his bare heel. He moved off into the thick purplish darkness of the tundra.

Brak disappeared slowly, growing smaller as he trudged away, a giant of a man naked save for the garment of lion's hide at his hips. Friar Jerome shielded his eyes against the reflection of the fire and watched.

He watched until Brak the barbarian was gone, lost there in the place where tundra and night horizon melted together, lost there among the white southern stars.

PART TWO

Flame Face

Break the chains!
Smash the walls!
Blood shall run in
Granite halls!

Lost were we,
Fettered kine,
Prisoned in
Uzhiram's mine

'Till a stranger,
Tall and free,
Struck his blow for
Liberty.

Broke the whips,
Laughed at fate,
Taught us how to
Howl with hate—

Toct shall fall!
Break her door!
Turn her streets to
Streams of gore!

Chaos comes!
Vengeance reigns!
*'Ware the slaves with
Shattered chains!*

—Song of the Toctish Rebellion

For fifty days and fifty nights Brak the barbarian had toiled now, a captive, down among the accursed in the ore mine of King Uzhiram of Toct.

He shared a foul cell that was one of a row of a hundred carved from the slimy stone that shone faintly emerald at night. His cell mate was a former caravaneer called Jath the Iramite.

The wiry little man had fallen into debt three years previously. He had bound himself voluntarily to labor in Uzhiram's mines in order to wipe his name from the debtors' roll and save himself from the headsman. He and the brawny wanderer with the long braid of yellow hair hanging down his mighty back got along well enough in their enforced intimacy. But Jath did not share Brak's boiling blood.

"You may fate yourself for worse than you've already got, barbarian."

Thus spoke Jath on the fifty-first night of Brak's imprisonment.

By the dim, evil glow of the moist rock walls the face of Brak was a study in furious frustration.

Using the small piece of granite which he kept hidden beneath his filthy pallet, he had just made a mark on the comparatively dry floor to indicate the passing of this fifty-and-first day of captivity. Now Brak sat with his back against the wall, employing the bit of granite to wear away at a link of strong black metal.

The link was one of a chain running between iron cuffs fastened to his ankles. The chain was short, so that Brak could take only hobbling steps. His hands remained free. But even a man as hot-tempered as Brak would not turn on his captors under such conditions. The big barbarian had seen a few men go mad and try, though. He and Jath and ten thousand others toiled in the smoky sulphurous warrens during endless sunless days, carrying reed baskets of raw reddish ore to the huge fire-lit chamber where the ores were melted.

"I'll take my risks tomorrow in any case," Brak growled at length. He had been working on the weakened link, grinding the bit of stone back and forth over it as quietly as he could, for the past twenty-two nights. "There are better things than swallowing your tongue when the Princess or her overseer lays on the lash. Even dying is a better thing."

Somewhere along the endless corridor onto which the rock pens opened, a prisoner shrieked in the grip of dementia. Guard boots slammed. A bolt was shot back. An argument ensued. The maniacal captive could not be silenced.

All at once, then, his burbling came sharply to a stop. Coarse laughter and the slower footfalls of the guards indicated that a dagger had served where blows and oaths would not. On more than one occasion the big barbarian had seen a troublemaker thus dispatched in the mines, his corpse flung into the glaring furnaces.

"What if you don't find freedom or even death, Brak, but life? Captivity again?" asked Jath.

Brak shrugged one brawny shoulder. "If I do? I'll not be worse off, will I?"

Jath shuddered. "You have heard the tales they tell."

Brak looked doubtful. "That below these levels where we work are other levels where the fires are ten times hotter and the horrors ten times worse? Aye, those things I've heard, and often. Probably they are lies put out by the overseers to forestall rebellions. What bottom of the pit could be blacker than this?"

Jath said nothing, sitting huddled and round-eyed in one corner. A guard in metal trappings passed outside, torch a-sputter. Quickly Brak bent his head over and appeared to doze. The guard peered through the spy hole in the thick door. Brak held his breath tight. Finally the guard passed on. The barbarian breathed deeply of the sulphurous air. It no longer bothered him as it first had on the day—or night? no telling down here—he had wakened, shouting and brawling, to find himself in chains.

After several minutes he picked up the bit of stone again. Steadily he worked away on the weak link. Every so often he would put down the rock and test the link by pulling the chain from both ends. Finally the link gave, nearly snapped. Brak growled under his breath. The sound could not be called a laugh. He tossed the bit of granite aside.

He sprawled on his back on the pallet, a savage figure, wide-shouldered and naked save for his garment of lion's hide about his hips. The garment he had been allowed to keep by the masters of the mine. His broadsword had been taken.

Through the nighttime stillness of the underground came a steady, far-off *hammer-clang, hammer-clang,* the sound of the forges making weapons of war for Vian, the Princess with the gold skin and cold purple eyes.

At length Jath cleared his throat and spoke: "Brak— my friend. I feel entitled to call you that."

"Yes," Brak replied. "'Twas you who first shared with me a cup of that slop that passes for broth, when none of the other prisoners would because I was an outlander."

"Then heed me. Do not try to escape tomorrow. You'll surely be caught and sent below." Dreadful horror crept into Jath's voice. "I have been here long enough to believe the tales. Especially that one which tells of the beast."

Brak looked dubious. "A six-legged creature taller than a man?"

"Doomdog has been a legend in the kingdom of Toct since time forgot. His image is carved on temple pillars.

That is, it was carved there until Princess Vian slew her uncle, King Uzhiram of Toct, with warlock-made poison daubed on the claws of his cockatoo. His body was spirited away so that none ever saw it, and the evil girl put on the coronet. Since then she has razed the temples, or so I understand from those prisoners who have arrived here within the last twelvemonth. But in the old days, the image of Doomdog was everywhere. Don't risk being condemned to the tunnels where it prowls."

Brak shrugged again, trying to feign an indifference which he did not feel. "I have seen monstrous creatures before, and fought them. I will do so again if that's the levy for my freedom."

Yet Jath had started Brak's mind imagining, and remembering. With horrid clarity, he recalled the awful events at the shrine of Yob-Haggoth. And he also recalled something else, which had taken place more recently.

Some days ago, he had been shuffling along with his ore basket in the human chain that ran continuously back and forth from where the ore was dug by purblind old men with mattocks to where it was dumped into heated vats. The endless file of men had passed a dark stair mouth leading downward. Moving with the line, Brak the barbarian had heard a distant, ugly rumbling from below. He recalled it now, vividly, and his backbone prickled with terror.

The noise from below had sounded like the monster roar of a cur dog, thundering as though caught by wind and blown into a sound a thousand times louder than normal. *Doomdog*—in the tunnels below.

And Brak remembered other things. From time to time the more rebellious prisoners were dragged away, never to reappear. And on occasion, the Princess Vian appeared in the mines with a party of fawning, elegantly-robed courtiers. She would select one or two prisoners who were then plucked forth by the guards and borne away. Where were they sent? Below? To Doomdog? Would he be dispatched similarly if he failed to make his escape?

"Please, barbarian," Jath began again. There was a strained catch in his voice. "Understand what I, as your friend, am trying to tell you."

"Then speak it plainly."

"I will be granted my freedom in another four-year."

"So you have told me several times, Jath. Because I am an outlander, I'm condemned to stay here the rest of my days, unless I do something about it."

"Don't think less of me if I—do not help you in the morning."

"I won't." Brak's voice was low, somber. "Sleep soundly on that."

"In truth you mean?"

"Jath, you have befriended me. I do not ask you to shed blood for me. I will take my own risks. But stay clear of me, for your own sake. The link in this leg chain is weak enough at last. I will not wait."

"Then I will pray to the gods of Tardam and Shargan that if you are overwhelmed, as you surely will be, that you take sword deep in your bowels and that it kills you, so that you will not be sent below."

Below... The word rang in Brak's mind like a great, dolorous bell pealing in a haunted waste. Quickly he turned his face to the wall so that Jath the Iramite could not see his expression of strain and uncertainty.

Through the darkness rang the *hammer-clang* of the forges, without cease. Since slaying her uncle and hiding his body away and usurping the throne, Princess Vian had sent her foot soldiers and her chariots (so it had been told to Brak), into all the neighboring kingdoms to make war and ravish the land. And though the mines were still called after the former lord of the land—Uzhiram's Mines—they served a more sinister ruler now.

Out of the mines in Uzhiram's time had come metals for the sword and spear that defended the land of Toct. Only criminals were sent to the mines, or debtors, self-bound like Jath. Now the mines teemed with political prisoners as well, and Princess Vian's overseers drove the captives at a merciless pace, for production needed to be tripled, quadrupled to sustain the armories of her war-making host.

Enough. He would not stay and die here. His destiny was a clear choice: either the road to golden Khurdisan, the dangerous but free road; or slow, fatal dying, in chains.

So on the morrow he would take his chances, and dice with death.

Brak's naked backbone shuddered in the creeping chill of night. His tan skin reflected the dim emerald radiance of the walls. Shortly he rolled over again. He could not sleep. The past made a shadow play of images in his mind.

The way on foot out of the Ice-marches had been arduous. Finally, however, Brak had come upon a crossroads caravanserai whose proprietor had been willing to take him on to do rough labor, outlander though he was. A period of months passed, at the end of which time Brak had saved up enough dinshas to purchase a pony to carry him south.

Thus Brak departed the crossroads, and a proprietor sorry to see him go, for Brak's brawny back made him an excellent worker, worth three ordinary men. Brak explained that he was bound to seek his fortune in the warmth of Khurdisan far southward, and rode out.

Some fifty-one days and nights ago, Brak had been riding his pony at a smart clip across an orange-sanded waste. He had been on the road the better part of a month, passing through desolate country. Because the land was barren, and he a stranger, he had never heard of Uzhiram, or Princess Vian, or the Toctish army's royal drill lands upon which he was unknowingly trespassing.

Toward sundown he cantered into a deserted oasis. As he was resting and watering the pony, a party of horsemen appeared on the horizon and swept down on him. These carrion turned out to be Princess Vian's Royal Blackbirders, slavers dignified by an impressive scroll bearing the mark of the Princess, new ruler of Toct.

Brak fought when they surged upon him. His broadsword chopped heads and limbs. But the slavers outweighed and outnumbered him. He was overwhelmed, and tried and convicted on the spot. The crime was trespassing.

Again Brak howled with rage, struggled to break loose, and was clubbed senseless.

He awoke in the mines of the murdered King Uzhiram, with iron circlets upon his ankles and black links between... Now one of the links was worn away. He would shatter it tomorrow.

Sound sleep still would not come. He lay drowsing uneasily, and once he thought he heard a grisly barking out of the depths of the earth. Then came a wild, forlorn moaning.

Some victim of Doomdog? he wondered. Or was it only Jath, strangely sobbing near at hand?

He must have slept, drifting in uneasy limbo where faceless foul things stirred and menaced him, for his awakening was abrupt and ugly. His eyes flew open. A raw stinging burned its way along his ribs on the right side, sending him rolling instinctively toward the wall. Someone had pricked his flesh cruelly with a spear tip.

Strange shimmering lights played near the half-open door leading to the rock corridor. Brak realized the lights were sputtering torches, with the gloom-warped figures of men looming behind them.

Hands seized his ankles. A voice cracked out: "See to the weak link so that we may know whether the informer spoke truth."

Brak recognized the voice of the night overseer of the prison corridor: a shallow-cheeked mercenary with a right eye that pointed crazily upward and away from his hooked nose. Other hands rattled the chain between Brak's ankles and bore down to pinion his lower legs.

Then came a second voice: "Aye, the link's nearly worn through."

"Hold him fast and fetch up the new irons," the overseer barked.

Brak's mind sang a single word. *Betrayal.*

Jath had been sobbing. Now the yellow-headed barbarian thought he knew why. He lay for only a heart's thud longer, letting them hold him. Fresh chains clinked in the corridor. Men shoved forward with the new shackles. Their torches glared on drawn broadswords. The overseer's bad eye stood out in flicker and shadow, moist and horrible, disembodied, suspended in space. Brak knew he could not wait.

Giving one violent swallow, he dragged his legs back, doubling them at the knees and toppling the men who had been holding him. Then he kicked out with all his strength.

The big barbarian's right foot caught the chin of one of the guards who had tumbled away a moment ago. The power of Brak's leg thews turned his foot into a juggernaut that snapped the man's head violently to the right. The mercenary's neck snapped even as he shrieked and writhed to his feet. In the confines of the cell, the cries touched off pandemonium.

Jerking up to a sitting position, Brak caught the bronze greave of the nearest guard, and tugged.

The man stumbled. Brak jumped up and wrenched the broadsword from the man's hand, using it to chop a great arc left to right.

At short range the stroke had tremendous force. The man's head fell from his neck and rolled. The headless body jetted blood that laved fierce and red over the barbarian.

Growling, animal-like, Brak thrust downward hard and at an angle. One stiff whack with the broadsword's edge and the weakened link snapped in half.

There was hesitation among the guards. The overseer howled, "Gut him! Gut the outlander, you weak-bellied worms!"

But fear held them off.

Brak was an awful sight, naked save for the lion hide, his ankles dragging chains as he charged, his wild yellow braid flying out, his sword arm springing back, then ramming forward.

The soldier nearest him could not parry in time. Brak's blade opened his bowels. The barbarian hauled his sword free of the corpse and kicked the body aside. He jumped across the ruin of the headless man and, turning swiftly, brought a stroke of vast power down across the nose of the next man in line.

The front half of the man's head was hacked open by the savage cut. Fresh blood gouted. Oaths, shrill yells of panic, the blundering of terrified men set up a fearsome din in the tiny cell.

Scenting freedom close, Brak closed both hands on the broadsword's haft and began to hew a red path toward the door.

Another guard perished. Another. Others jabbed their spears at him, but more cautiously now, edging away from him into the corridor. In the other cells prisoners had set up a maniacal clamor of encouragement, approval.

The cast-eyed overseer let his soldiers fight while he scuttled to the left along the corridor. Parrying the lunge of a swag-bellied guard, Brak saw the overseer reach an alcove where a hanging lanthorn swayed. The overseer caught a thong attached to the clapper of a large bell hung from the ceiling. Wildly he yanked the thong back and forth. The alarm pealed and echoed in the warrens of the mine.

Panting, Brak lowered his broadsword. The three guards remaining alive were retreating toward the overseer and the bell. Brak could not flee in that direction. He spun half around.

Beyond the overseer, metal flashed in the torch light. More troops were coming in answer to the bell's clangor. The cell corridor stretched into sinister gloom in the other direction. Brak had no idea of his position in the mine, but his choice was clear: either remain and be slain by superior numbers; or flee and take his chances in mazy darkness.

He chose the latter alternative, sucking in great draughts of air as he slammed down the line of cells, using his free hand to shoot open as many door bolts as he could.

The stumbling, weakened derelicts tottered into the light, fearful at first. But by the time there were two dozen of them freed and milling behind Brak as he ran, they had begun to chant and roar with anger. They formed a human wall between the barbarian and his pursuers.

The soldiers arrived. They started fighting and hacking their way through the freed prisoners, who fought fiercely with their fists. A spear snaked past Brak's shoulder as he flung open one more cell door.

Another spear grazed his flank. About to plunge into the unknown dark beyond the point where the cells stopped, Brak stumbled against a hulking figure.

"Brak?" The voice piped in fear. "Brak, you must understand why—"

The barbarian's trembling left hand caught the man's throat. *"Jath!"*

"Understand," the Iramite wept, "understand why I crept to the door and called the overseer as you slept. I bargained. They said they would remit the four-year that I have left to service and make me a free man!" His voice keened up as he seized Brak's gore-streaked forearm. "I sent myself here but it has been a hateful, accursed life. I could not bear any more of it. This was my only chance! I tried to persuade you not to try to escape. You wouldn't heed me. I knew I might weaken, tell them. You wouldn't heed. *I couldn't help what I did.*"

Howling, Jath the Iramite stumbled backward along the dimly glowing rock wall. A cold, powerful draught swirled around Brak's legs suddenly. His right arm shook with violent tremors. He drew his right arm back to kill the man who had betrayed him.

Never before had Brak slain a man who had not threatened him first. But his mind was racing out of control.

Behind him prisoners clogged the corridor. The soldiers could not fight their way through. They hurled more spears.

One pricked Brak's shoulder blade, dug a runnel out of flesh, spun off to clank against the far wall.

The darts of pain maddened the big barbarian even more. Whirling, he scooped up the spear with the hand he had freed from Jath's throat. He hurled the spear hard.

Just breaking through the clutch of rioting prisoners, the overseer caught its metal head in his belly. The overseer danced backward, trying to pluck out the shaft. He sprawled into a pack of the prisoners. They fell on him like clawing steppe wolves.

Turning back, the barbarian took a harder grip on his broadsword and peered ahead into the deceptive darkness of the corridor.

On his left, still feeling his way along the wall, Jath moved hunched over, hampered by his clinking leg chain. Brak shambled after him, broadsword hanging from his bloody hand.

The darkness thickened. The area of cells was lost behind. Only torchlight from back there helped Brak locate the darker patch of shadow that was his betrayer. The biting air struck his face and chest, stinking as though it rose from the center of the earth.

"Let me alone," Jath whimpered. *"Let me alone."* Then, shrieking past Brak: "Overseer, help me! You promised to protect..."

"Crazy-eye won't hear you," Brak growled. "I gutted him with a spear."

With one swift leap Brak closed the distance between them. Just as his free hand fastened on Jath's throat, the Iramite flailed wildly. He had been backing up, along the wall, and now suddenly there was no wall to support him. There was only a stygian opening.

Brak crashed against Jath as the man howled in fear and fell backwards through the opening, dragging the barbarian with him.

Falling, tumbling in sickening emptiness, Brak knew moments of blind terror. Then his back struck shaly rock. It angled downward. He shot out a hand to try to stop himself, could not. Over and over he tumbled, knocked, whacked, battered.

He rolled faster and faster down a slope tunneled within the rock. A slope, his agonized mind told him, like others in the mine, up which ore carts were hauled by winch chains. This one, apparently, was abandoned.

Somewhere below a reddish glare rose. Brak barely managed to hang on to his broadsword and keep its cutting edge turned away from his flesh as he tumbled over and over. A rock banged his head. Another gouged his backbone. Still he kept rolling down the abandoned slope, hearing somewhere ahead Jath's moan.

The glare increased, flaring outward to engulf him. Bruised, hurt, Brak pitched suddenly from the tunnel into an open place filled with the blood-hued light.

He sprawled onto solid rock which was hot to the touch. He came rolling and twisting to a stop against a sodden hulk. He dragged himself to his hands and knees and looked at the hulk. His eyes grew less blurred. The hulk slowly took on definition.

It was Jath the Iramite. The life had been crushed out of the man's frail form by the long fall. Jath's neck had snapped. His head lolled at a twisted angle. His eyes bulged, reflecting fire. His tongue protruded between clenched teeth.

Horror-struck, Brak breathed a prayer to nameless gods on the poor wretch's behalf. Then, from the corner of his eye he caught a strange shimmer and glanced toward it.

He bit down upon his bottom lip until he tasted the salt of blood in his mouth. There lay his broadsword, its blade aglitter with the reflection of *a face made of fire.*

Slowly Brak clambered to his feet. He turned full around. His eyes flew wide. The great room hewn from the rock at the bottom of the earth stretched into near-limitless dark on every hand. Across its floor was strewn the effluvia of past suffering: rusted mine carts, rotting wooden trestles, caved-in smelting equipment, and bleached bones scattered like a white salt. Two corpses in the foreground looked fresher, some gobbets were left on the skeletons. Rats of immense size, with glittering eyes, chittered and scampered in and out among the picked rib cages until a clink of Brak's ankle chains sent them scurrying into the dark.

But Brak's gaze was drawn past all this to an immense arch in the far wall. Beyond it, as though springing up from subterranean furnaces, great bonfire tongues of flame leaped, scorching hot, turning the rock floor beneath his feet to blistering heat.

Suspended by wrist-ropes in the heart of this conflagration directly beyond the arch hung a bearded ancient, a half-seen thing with limbs, robe, and head wreathed in fire.

The thing's beard was flame tongued. Its hair writhed in tendrils of light and smoke. Yet a human form was discernible. The mouth writhed as though in exquisite agony. Even across the distance of the chamber, Brak could see that its all too human eyes were open... Open and *staring*.

It was an old, old man suspended in a holocaust of fire. His rope bindings did not burn; his garments did not burn; his beard and hair did not burn; and yet he was all afire, suspended in the flame and a part of it, burning, burning but never dying.

Laughter came like delicate bells.

"Another guest," said a lilting feminine voice. "Quite by accident, it seems. Well, he may enjoy the sight we show to those we select to be our guests down here."

Within the furnace the prisoned creature writhed at the end of its ropes, its mouth opening and shutting as if in cries of torment. Brak thought he heard a faint moan as, numbly, he turned in the direction of the feminine voice.

Shadows stirred on the chamber's far side. There was a clinking of armor. Several figures separated from darkness, becoming defined as they moved forward. Brak glimpsed helmets, breastplates, the livid faces of half-a-dozen soldiers with narrow, gem-encrusted blades drawn.

The courtiers formed a ring around the girl who had spoken. She moved forward also, clad in pearl-sewn white slippers and a mist of rich purple cloaks.

Out of Brak's mouth came a grunt of wonderment and fury: "Vian."

"Call her by her proper title, filth," one of the courtiers yelled.

The girl stood there, golden skin deepened by the firelight but her purple eyes were colder than the great glaciers Brak had ridden across in perilous winters. The girl laid a bangled hand on the wrist of the nearest courtier.

"Ease a moment, Radoran," said Princess Vian. Her mouth was moist, sweetly smiling, tempting as a poisoned fruit. "This one I have seen on those occasions when I have plucked a political prisoner out of the mine cells. He is an outlander. Look at the lionskin, the blood all over him. He and his dead companion lying there must have fallen down the old incline in a foolish attempt to escape." She raised her voice slightly. "Barbarian? How are you called?"

The words spat out: "Brak is my name, hell-woman."

The courtiers surged forward again. The Princess restrained them. And now that his eyes were becoming accustomed to the red glare, he could see beyond the little group. He noted several details; cloth-of-gold carpets spread on the rock; silver ewers and viand baskets nearby; and still deeper in the dark, a muted, sickly-yellow torch hanging in a socket above a staircase cut from the chamber's wall... Where did the staircase lead?

"Well, my wild man Brak from somewhere," the Princess mocked, "you have surprised us on our outing. Our guest went into the furnace only a a few moments ago. He was a former adviser to my uncle. Brought not from the mines this time, but directly from the palace by that more direct, secret route," indicating the staircase. "Before our guest died, we showed him the prized possession of our regency. There."

She flung out a bangled arm. Brak turned, awestruck, for her face was etched in evil despite its youthful beauty as she pointed at the writhing apparition within the monster furnace.

"There, barbarian. There hangs my dear Uncle Uzhiram. Neither alive nor dead. His body is not harmed by the hottest fires of his own mines. Yet he is never released from the unending torment that burns and *burns and burns him.*"

Her voice had dropped low, vile with madness. Sweat on her face made her beauty a mockery. Dimly now, Brak understood: "I heard that the King's body was never found.

"For a reason, dear guest. My uncle was enchanted by my warlocks just at the moment the poison from the cockatoo's claws coursed through his being; the fleeting moment before his life flickered out. He was enchanted and hung up down here to feel the pain of fire forever. And there you see him, a source of pleasure to me, and fitting final sight for those traitors, caught and uncaught, whom I must gradually remove from the palace and the mines."

"You show your enemies—this?" Brak's tone was rich with loathing.

"Aye," she replied merrily. "'Tis quite sobering."

"And you make an outing of it?"

"Yes. You glimpsed the food and the wine things, then."

"I did," he choked back. "The whole thing is a filthy cruelty."

"To a barbarian, perhaps. 'Tis not to me."

"How can prisoners in the mine harm you?"

"There are rebellious men among them."

Brak wondered what transpired on the levels above, where he had left the freed prisoners brawling with the guards. He could not comprehend the thinking of the Princess. "But they are in chains. Why torment them?"

"Oh," she answered with a shrug, setting the diamond-crusted rings of her cape-fastenings to jingling and winking with white pinpoints, "because it gives me pleasure. When I release them to bring them down here, I always make a promise of clemency. Then I show them my Uncle Uzhiram and let their hopes go crashing."

The courtier Radoran had developed a strange twitching in one cheek. His head swiveled, as if he were listening. Brak swayed a moment, then rubbed his eyes. The rock burned beneath his naked soles. He was weakened by the terrific pounding he'd absorbed on the long fall down the slope, and only with difficulty did he attune his ears to catch the noise that had alarmed the courtier.

A mixture of sounds congealed in Brak's ear: far away, an awful, sustained roar, nearer at hand, somewhere in the dark to his right, a heavy, menacing pant of breathing, a frightening *scrape-and-scratch*. Brak isolated the source of the former noise. It was an answer to his mental question of moments ago, about the fate of the prisoners.

The roar issued from the crumbling mouth of the inclined tunnel down which he'd fallen. Radoran identified the same source almost simultaneously.

"Princess, we must haste back up the staircase to the horses, and ride for the palace. There's tumult in the mines."

"Men crying for freedom," Brak said. "And striking for it. I loosed them."

Princess Vian licked her lips as the fire-glare washed over her twisted face. "Then, Radoran, since the outlander admits his guilt, we must punish him."

"But Princess, we should not delay when…"

"We shall delay! You will catch the barbarian on spears and lift him out into the furnace. Of a sudden, his face and his swagger disgust me."

"Princess," another courtier whispered, "we beg you to listen to Radoran. The outlander's limbs stink of blood. And blood will bring the—"

Annnngghhhh.

Terror crystalized in Brak's mind. The inhuman, ear-hurting moan of anguish had issued from the flame-wreathed mouth of the enchanted King hanging within the furnace. Once more it came. *Annnngghhhh.*

Brak turned to see the flame-figure twist, roasting at the end of its ropes, yet never burning, never dying. Again and again the moan was repeated, filling the whole of the underground chamber while the face of King Uzhiram seemed to turn toward the barbarian standing there, gore-stained sword in his hand, as if he were a deliverer.

And then, even louder than the hideous moaning, came a new grinding, panting horror of sound that turned Brak around still one more time. This time it was to face the beast-thing that snuffled and crept from blackness on its six long-clawed feet.

A vile-bulbous head sat on immense shoulders. The head itself was three times wider than a man was tall. Immense, slavering jaws click-clocked open and shut as the thing halted, swiveling its head. Obviously it was searching for the source of the blood-smell.

Its baleful milky-colored eyes rolled like balls of mist within its head. The foul-odored fur of its body seemed to bristle and ripple as slowly, slowly, the monster's head dipped and turned and the ebony-wet muzzle distended.

Blood-smell had brought the Doomdog hunting. It scented the big barbarian all at once. It ticked the claws of its middle right leg on stone. With ponderous steps it began to advance.

Brak took a hard grip on his broadsword haft. The thing's ghastly red tongue lolled from its head, water dripping off and splashing into huge pools were it walked. Cautiously Brak began to take backward steps. One... Two... Three...

The Doomdog stalked him, sure of its strength. Princess Vian and her trembling courtiers huddled in a group. Of them all, only the girl watched with interest, with death-lust and no fear on her face.

Of a sudden, as Brak backed up, his left foot went down on something coldly tubular. It rolled under his naked instep. He windmilled his arms, pumping for balance, and fell.

He fell backward. Everything spun around him. He had a tortured glimpse of the long, bleached thigh bone that had caused him to stumble. Unbearable heat fanned his naked back.

Wildly his left hand stabbed out, fingers closing and clawing around rock. He dug in his heels. His whole arm ached as he hung braced by it, his back and head angled out over the flames of the furnace. He had nearly tumbled backward through the arch, and had caught himself on the left-hand edge of the archway just in time.

Carefully, carefully, he adjusted the weight on the soles of his feet. With a quick pull, he jerked erect, struggled to balance himself. The backs of his heels still hung out over emptiness, flame.

Directly behind him the ghoulish specter of the ever-burning, King Uzhiram swayed faintly in the sulphurous updrafts from the pit of flame. The victim's moaning filled Brak's ears with a tormented thunder.

But the big barbarian could ill afford to rip his eyes away from the monster bearing down on him with measured steps. Somehow the Doomdog sensed that the barbarian had accidentally worked himself into a position in which he was trapped, flames at his back. The Doomdog began to pant faster, its misshapen head waggling back and forth as it advanced and closed the distance.

Suddenly it broke into a swift charge, moving with fantastic speed. Over Brak's head yawned the wet red maw and the huge teeth, as the head dipped downward to bite and kill and swallow him.

The yellow-headed barbarian dropped to all fours and crawled between the pairs of the Doomdog's legs. He rolled and twisted and sprang up, ramming his broadsword high over his head with two hands and striking once, twice, three times, four, deep into the Doomdog's underbelly.

From the ripped wounds a thick, tainted white ichor began to drip and plop. The Doomdog dug its claws into the stone, striking sparks that flew against Brak's skin and burned. The Doomdog had pulled itself to a halt on the lip of the rock floor just at the arch, so that now it had to turn to search for the attacker bedeviling it with swordbites from beneath.

Brak struck upward again, again. The ichor was raining around him. The Doomdog's underbelly strained in and out, threatening to crush the barbarian as he dodged back and forth, stabbing.

Then, dimly, Brak realized that his strategy might be his undoing. The monster was bellowing in pain, giving great yelping barks that shook the rock walls of the cavern. It was hurt, perhaps mortally.

One of its legs skidded wildly, as though its strength had suddenly ebbed. If all those legs gave way at once, Brak would be crushed beneath the falling hulk.

Blood and ichor smearing him from head to foot, the yellow-headed barbarian turned and charged for the beast's right foreleg. Taking a last, desperate double-handed grip on the broadsword haft, he hammered the blade with all his power against the back of that foreleg.

He hacked open the Doomdog's fibrous hide to the bone. Ichor gouted, and Brak sensed rather than saw above him the sudden collapse of the monster's gigantic body. He hurled himself to the right.

The Doomdog was falling, a black sky descending. Brak seemed unable to move fast enough. The Doomdog's monster bulk was tumbling down on top of him, down, down, blotting out everything, the cavern, Princess Vian, the redness, the hanging King.

Twisting, writhing, Brak hit the scorching stone as the Doomdog collapsed. Brak's left foot was caught beneath the hideous weight of the beast. He shrieked aloud in pain and dragged it free.

The Doomdog's bulbous head hung over the fire-pit, the hair singeing, sparking, smoldering. Then, with a fearsome whimper, the Doomdog dragged its forelegs up beneath it, attempting to stand.

The foreleg that Brak had slashed gave way, the paw slipping off the pit's edge.

With a growl and roar that shook the earth, the Doomdog slid over into the leaping flames. As it fell, its milky eyes searched for the source of its torment. It saw the flame-wreathed body of King Uzhiram hanging. It snapped its dying jaws around the King as it fell.

Ropes and tackle pulled out of the roof of the furnace pit. Blocks of stone and mortar gave way in a tremendous thundering roar. The Doomdog dropped down, down into the flames, other flames streaking from its clamped-shut mouth.

King Uzhiram was gone. The Doomdog was gone. From the depths of the furnace there came a sudden vast up-pouring of purple fire, a smashing explosion that hurled Brak skidding along the rock.

Then came silence.

Dazed, bleeding, nearly senseless, Brak hauled himself up on one knee. His fingers twitched toward the haft of his fallen broadsword as footsteps rustled, voices whispered.

The courtiers, Brak thought. He saw winking blades in his fogged brain. *Beware the courtiers.*

He heard a clicking and raised his head. The courtiers were fleeing up the great staircase along the far wall. Closer to hand, small fists clenched at her sides, Princess Vian shook with rage.

"Radoran! Martix! You filthy cowards. It makes no difference that Uzhiram is gone! My power is the same. Come back! *My power is the same. It is not diminished.*"

The courtiers believed otherwise. Terror had driven them away because her talisman, the enchanted flame-corpse, no longer hung in the arch. And with it, perhaps, had gone the strongest source of her authority over the fearful minds of the men who followed her.

Princess Vian's right cheek shone with something crystal-bright. A tear?

Brak stumbled to his feet. He shook his head and rubbed his bleeding palms on the lion-hide at his waist.

"I am glad," he said slowly, "that I am an outlander, with no friends among civilized men. Their courage is like a glass bauble. Empty and worthless."

"Stand away from me," Princess Vian whispered. "I still rule here."

Brak's cracked lips peeled away from his teeth in a hideous smile. "I think not, little Princess of blood. Listen."

Up the incline leading to the mine, a clamor of voices rose stronger. It was a chant of freedom being ripped from others by force. It was the cry of ten-thousand slaves let loose.

Even now firefly torches winked in the portion of the angled tunnel which Brak could see. He chuckled deep in his huge, aching chest as half-a-dozen blinking prisoners in filthy tunics leaped and scrambled down the incline, firebrands raised high. The men carried swords and spears, freshly red at the tips. One of them saw Brak.

"Yonder! The outlander. The one who was prisoned with us."

"And see who's with him," said another hoarsely. Hate brimmed in his voice. "The usurper of Uzhiram's throne."

"She is a prisoner," Brak said.

On slippered feet Princess Vian ran to him. She huddled against him, then raised her face and looked into his eyes. Her hands crawled on his body. She pleaded: "Kill me."

Brak was silent.

"Please. Kill me yourself."

Brak hesitated. Red rage washed high in him. It slowly diminished. "No," he growled. "That right belongs to the men who have carried the day in the mine above."

Leaning down, he caught up his reddened broadsword in one fist, slung the girl over his shoulder with the other hand and began to walk toward the ex-slaves with the torches. From up the incline came the sound of jubilation.

Princess Vian lay against him, golden flesh cold, immobile. Halfway to the slaves, Brak turned aside. He walked into the darkness to the site of the grisly outing. Silver ewers gleamed on cloth-of-gold spread upon the hot stone. Butts of meat and scraps of bread lay all about.

With a snarl Brak kicked over the tallest silver ewer and watched its rich purple contents gush forth onto the gold cloth, staining it. Princess Vian sobbed once. When the last of the wine had trickled out, Brak raised his foot. He crushed it down on the ewer, bending the vessel into a shapeless scrap.

Then he turned and carried his burden toward the ragged men with the torches and the merciless eyes.

PART THREE

The Courts
of the Conjurer

Touch not the Silks of Shaitan, Prince,
For filthy gods have spun them well.
And haunted each with fearsome pow'r
To suck thy heart straight down to hell.

—*The Abominable Wisdoms of Lady Yrain,* xxxii

Hall opened onto great, brooding hall as the strange little procession of four went to answer the summons. In each succeeding hall, the sense of evil grew.

The big yellow-haired barbarian scowled. A breeze tugged at the edge of the splendid silken cloak which Lord Tazim had bid him wear as part of the scheme. His single long and savage braid was hidden beneath a high-wrapped headpiece of cloth-of-gold. In all respects, down to the kidskin boots with curling toes, he was garbed identically with the scrawny, obviously awe-struck retainer who marched beside him, but whose name Brak did not know.

A puny, worthless blade in the shape of a crescent moon hung from the barbarian's ruby-studded belt. He longed for his own mighty broadsword, the one the blood-maddened rebels of Toct had give him as a token of comradeship. But the broadsword was concealed back among the pearls and opals, the sapphires and enameling and silverwork, in one of the chests containing the dowry of Princess Jarmine.

The dowry chests had been left behind in a sumptuous apartment. Yet for all practical purposes, they already belonged to the overlord of this vast, opulent and weirdly deserted collection of spires, battlements and courts perched on a basalt outcrop above the pass that led through the mountains. They would belong to the overlord of this place, unless Brak made up his mind to play the assassin.

"'*Ware*." The jeweled robes of the middling-aged, stern-faced Tazim winked in torch glare. "There's a brighter glimmering ahead. At last perhaps we can meet this bragging bandit who invited us in to be robbed."

"I wish he had a few courtiers with lyres, whoever he is," said the supple, lovely girl walking beside the older man.

Her feet and hands were delicate, her hair a copper shimmer, her mouth as ripe looking as the orchard's fruit. But she had a whining and petulant way about her which Brak had disliked from the first.

The girl continued: "There are only empty chambers and a few surly guards in this place. I will say that the furnishings give the lord the look of a wealthy man. Otherwise his domain's as dull as that belonging to Omer, the poor clod. My sisters have said it's a sleepy kingdom Omer rules, anyway."

"Stop your clack, Jarmine." Tazim was curt. "'Tis unseemly to speak of your intended, the Prince, in such fashion."

"I'm not the one who arranged the match, Father!" The girl's pale white gown rustled in the fitful night breeze.

Borne by that breeze came a stink such as Brak had never smelled before during his wanderings in the so-called civilized world. The nauseating aroma, as of a wharf and charnel house mingling their taints, seemed to drift up from a vast pool. The pool occupied the center of the roofless court that they were entering.

Just a lone torch flickered in the high mountain wind, along the colonnade. Despite this the court was remarkably full of light. An unearthly radiance seemed to rise from the depths of the pool, on the surface of which sweet-scented petals floated by the hundreds.

No flower petals could mask the stench pouring up from that pool, though, Brak thought. It was a death stench.

Lord Tazim and his lovely daughter were already hurrying ahead toward a further arch. Beyond it, oil lamps gleamed. As Brak the barbarian and the frightened retainer kept pace, there was a ripple, then a splash.

Tense throughout his still-aching body, Brak swung his head. He blinked, as if to drive out dreams. Petals bobbed gently on the water. For the merest space of time, Brak had been positive he had seen something frightful beneath the surface—a great tusklike whiteness, distorted by the water, quick to disappear.

"Don't stand goggling," whispered the creature at his left. "The Lord was a fool to bring us into this accursed place. And he was doubly foolish to persuade you to help him. No man, not even a lawless outlander, could…"

One of Brak's brawny arms thrust out. He was beginning to get a bellyful once again of the civilities and courtesies of those who were, supposedly, the opposite of barbaric. Brak's powerful fingers closed around the retainer's wattled throat.

"Not one word," Brak whispered.

"Let me go," the man cheeped, wriggling.

"Yes, I will. But make any sign to reveal that I don't belong to your Lord's pack of retainers and this toy of a sword they gave me can probably slit your stomach open before it snaps."

"I—I'll say nothing," the man quavered. Brak let him go. The retainer rubbed his throat. "What the Lord could have offered you to go through with this mummery I can't imagine."

Brak scowled. "What do you mean?"

"A fortune wouldn't be enough to pay a sane man to be here. I have no choice. But you, didn't you see? In that pool a moment ago… gods, I don't know what it was. But it swam there, alive, and it—"

At the far arch, Lord Tazim called, "Lift your feet, you oafs. Promptly."

Ah, thought Brak with mingled fury and fear. There had been something unnamed and awful in that pool beneath the high mountain stars. Well, whatever it was, he'd face it. He'd struck a bargain with Tazim.

The Lord had offered him balm for his back, burial for the Nestorian Brak was unable to save, and a cart to carry off the butcherwork done to the splendid pony that the new rebel governors of Toct had awarded him. Tazim had also promised him half the contents of the dowry chests.

Brak distrusted the offer of all that wealth. On the other hand, it might carry him far and more smoothly on the road to Khurdisan, with less difficulty than he had encountered thus far.

The only contingency upon which Brak's reward depended was that he do murder.

Tazim, Lord of the Tilling, was thus called because of his penchant for agriculture and peaceful rule in his domain at the mountain's foot. Tazim knew the master of this eyrie only by reputation. To test the superstitious legend, Tazim had taken the direct route through the mountain pass, rather than a longer way. His purpose was to deliver his daughter as a bride to one Prince Omer, who lived in Kopt on the mountain's far side.

For a lord of peaceable repute, Brak thought, Tazim concealed a rare courage beneath his mild mien. Brak had met the Lord in perilous circumstances.

After the successful rebellion of the Toctish miners, and the establishment of a people's rule to replace that of the depraved Princess Vian, Brak had lingered in Toct a month, resting and taking his pleasure until he grew weary of the fights and the adulation that the old Uzhiram loyalists had heaped upon him. At length he departed for the south. The call of Khurdisan still was strong in his blood, as he knew it would always be until he reached his destination.

After several days of uneventful traveling he rode into the land ruled by Tazim, Lord of the Tilling. At a caravanseri, hangers-on warned him of the menace that made the pass through the mountains unsafe. Yes, they did agree that this route was the shortest to Kopt and the south, but they advised...

Brak left them scratching their beards in puzzlement as he rode away with his broadsword slapping his flank. From their expressions, they thought him a madman to take such a beclouded route.

As Brak was taking the trail up into the mountains, he chanced upon another pilgrim, a priest of Nestoriamus. Brak was suspicious of the man's religion, but he vividly recalled the kindness with which Friar Jerome had treated him during their awful encounter with Septegundus in the Ice-marches. So Brak made courteous conversation with the priest, and they rode on up into the mountains together. The priest was on his way to convert the heathens of Kopt.

They were soon set upon by four of the riders who served the mysterious ruler of the pass. One of the riders pulled the priest's cross from its cord and spat upon it. Another demanded Brak's pony and the few dinshas in his pouch. The barbarian drew his broadsword.

Numbers were against him. Soon both Brak and the Nestorian were roped by their thumbs from a cypress limb, then whipped unmercifully and left to die.

Only the huge barbarian, with his immense resources of strength, was still breathing when Lord Tazim's small train came tinkling up the trail in a scarlet sundown. Tazim, too, despite warnings, had chosen the most direct route to Kopt.

His retainers cut down the dead priest and buried him. They also dug a pit for the slaughtered remains of Brak's pony. From among Tazim's supplies came balm for Brak's whip marks.

The following dawn, the campsite was visited by three new outriders bearing a demand from their master, plus an invitation to discuss the terms as guests of the ruler of the pass. When the horsemen rode away, Tazim approached Brak at the campfire. The barbarian was gnawing on a greasy bone of beef.

"None of my people has ventured though this pass since I was a small child, barbarian," Tazim began.

Brak put down the bone. "So, Lord?"

"We had no need. The tales drifting down from these peaks have been grim over the years. At our hostels we warn the traveler to follow the longer river trail around the mountain spur."

"Yes, I was so warned."

"The first two parties of emissaries from Prince Omer of Kopt climbed the pass but never reached my border. 'Twas with the third such party, which came the long way around, that I struck the bargain for Jardine."

"Why are you telling me all this?"

"So that you understand the menace of these mountains."

"If you knew such a menace existed, why didn't you take soldiers and wipe it out?"

"For generations, barbarian, we've thrived with no army to speak of in my land. You said you had ridden through. Did you see soldiers anywhere?"

"No, only farmers and herdsmen."

"I am a peaceful man. Even so, the time has come for strength. I will not be frightened off by a mountain bandit who cloaks himself in superstition. I have brought my daughter and her dowry this way of my own choice."

Brak grunted. This Tazim had courage despite his mild way of speaking.

"I have come this way," the Lord continued, "and found you, amid a scene of hopeless, heartless butchery."

"The lord of the pass deserves to have an army hammer down his gates and gut him," Brak agreed.

"But I have no army. You will have to be my army if we cannot reason with the master of those riders."

"Me? I am only one man."

"A strong-looking man, though. Is there no thirst in you for revenge?"

Brak thought of the dead Nestorian, of his pony, of the way the riders had laid on the lash to his naked back.

"Yes, I have a strong thirst that way, Lord."

"Very well. I offer you half the contents of the dowry chests if I decide to have the bullying creature who rules this pass killed."

Brak reflected a moment. "And what will decide you?" "Why, merely whether he persists in the demands made by that trio of horsemen who just rode off. Namely, that I surrender to him all the dowry intended for Omer of Kopt who is to marry my daughter." A flinty light gleamed in the nobleman's eyes. "Turnabout. What will decide you whether you will kill him for me, outlander?"

"Why," Brak echoed uneasily, "how he in turn treats you." "There may be considerable danger," Tazim said.

"Aye. But you are going."

"I must. Else we will never be permitted to leave this savage place at all."

"At the caravanseri, there were tales—"

Tazim's eyes narrowed. "That the master of the pass has

awful powers at his command? Indeed, I have often heard them, as I intimated. I do not know their truth. We will have to learn for ourselves one way or another. Well?"

With another grunt, Brak rose from his haunches in the chill dawn air. "A bargain. I'll go."

"Splendid. Come, we will see to outfitting you."

Moving along toward the arch now, Brak felt a twinge of conscience. He really had no use for ass-loads of pearls and sapphires. A full pouch of dinshas would speed his travel south toward the warm climes of Khurdisan, but as for accepting more, Brak was not certain that he could.

What drove him most of all was the bloodthirst for revenge.

Suddenly a gong sounded, its weird note shivering away to silence. Brak scratched his side. He was uncomfortable in the accoutrements of a courtier.

"Please be welcome in my modest home," said a voice beyond the arch through which Tazim and his daughter were just passing. Brak and the other retainer hurried ahead.

The chamber beyond the arch was large, high-ceilinged and relatively well lit. Brak and the retainer, who was shuddering now, entered and moved to the left, hanging back against the rear wall. No armed guards were visible anywhere. Though this should have comforted Brak, it did not. Other circumstances lent an ominous note.

Tazim and Jardine approached a dais. The man who had spoken rose from a round, low-backed throne. To its right stood a filigreed taboret on which rested an ebony casket, medium-small, its sides and curved top glittering in torch light.

To the left of the dais, hundreds of strangely veined, shining black rocks were piled up in a bizarre pyramid. While some were slightly smaller than others, all had roughly the same unusual shape.

"If you have no objection," said Tazim haughtily, "may we dispense with the formalities? Other than your name, of course. Your true name. I dislike dealing with anonymous thieves."

From the shadowed place where he watched, Brak saw the figure on the dais stiffen. The man was sallow skinned. He had thinnish cheeks, a tuft of beard. His eyes were mocking, black as his little cask or the robe which belled about his feet. In a certain light, he might have passed for a young, handsome adventurer. At close range, there was an unhealthy, flaccid quality about his skin which somehow told Brak that the man was older than old.

The man touched the tips of his ringed fingers together. "A thief? Is it wrong to extract a price for passage across one's own land? Ah, well. That's a quibble. But anonymous? That, I am sure, cannot be the case. Don't the louts in your kingdom know my name, Lord?"

"Some call you a wizard," was Tazim's reply. "A practitioner of the hellish arts, a sorcerer. I don't believe a word of it."

Two tiny spots of scarlet appeared in the man's whey cheeks. "My name is Ankhma Ra, and thus you will address me.

Tazim snorted. "I am not accustomed to accepting orders from—"

Ankhma Ra whirled down from the dais suddenly, startling Tazim into silence. "Curb your stupid tongue if you want this pretty little minx to reach her betrothed in Kopt beyond this pass. I ask the dowry chests as payment for passage, and I will get them. Is it not better than throwing away your lives?"

In dismay Brak watched the copper-haired Princess. Her head was cocked at a curious angle. Her cheeks were flushed as she gazed at the spindly man called Ankhma Ra. She spoke with a certain tone of perverse admiration: "He has a quick tongue, Father. Few men would dare call you down that way. He also seems to have accumulated enough wealth in this place to prove— well, perhaps that his threats are not entirely idle."

So furious was Tazim, his gnarled brown hands knotted at his sides. But he spoke no reply. Ankhma Ra bowed to the Princess.

"Thank you, little one. You are a perceptive child. And a most fetching one, too."

Tazim did not miss the girl's sudden, wanton flush, nor Ankhma Ra's low laugh.

"You addle-pated little strumpet!" Tazim whispered. "Of all my daughters, 'tis you who have been a plague to me all my life."

Never had Brak seen a girl shrug in a more cruel or callous way, as if to say that it mattered little. Ankhma Ra strode quickly to the cask on the taboret. He laid a long-nailed hand atop it.

"Shall we come to the point? The dowry chests or no?"

Tazim glared. "I will not even deign to answer such a presumptuous—"

"I am not a man of infinite patience," the other interrupted again. "Don't imagine you can simply leave at your leisure, even though I did invite you as my guests so that you might ponder the alternatives. Should you think of swords, of your retainers, two of whom I see hulking back there, my men, though few in number, are loyal. They know the passages in this place while your men do not. They would like nothing better than feeding morsels to the amusing creature I keep in the pool. No one knows how deep that pool runs, incidentally. Perhaps to hell itself. I have a certain adeptness with natural substances, among other things, and from the earlier generations of creatures in that pool, I have managed to breed—but no need to dwell on that. Suffice it to say the Fangfish is hungry."

The Fangfish.

Brak's palms turned clammy. Underneath the blue surface of the water, he had seen something loathsome, darting away. Tusk or fang, it had been as long as a man was tall.

"There is a simpler way," Ankhma Ra continued, opening the black sack. He pointed.

Like a red flower, a scarlet silk way balled within the cask. The fabric seemed to shift and modulate from shade to shade of red.

Said Tazim, "I've already had a bellyful of this tawdry marketplace performance. You try to frighten grown men with a simple kerchief of—*ah!*"

Tazim's cry was sharp, pained. The Lord had been reaching out for the shimmering silk. Ankhma Ra had struck his hand away with great force.

"Do not pose as an authority on things you know nothing about," said the dark-bearded man. Carefully he drew from either side of the silk a pair of immense iron gauntlets. Into the red-velvet linings of these he fitted his hands. Only then did Ankhma Ra lift the bit of scarlet, toss it up and catch it again.

In bazaars along his route, Brak had often seen conjurers do tricks with silks. Yet never before had he laid eyes on a silk whose very texture seemed constantly mottling, shifting, altering between ghastly shades and tints of red. It seemed alive.

Ankhma Ra walked past Lord Tazim and the copper-haired girl. He approached Brak and the other retainer.

"The Silks of Shaitan are ancient," Ankhma Ra murmured. "Very rare. I am privileged to possess one, this one. To lift it with my bare hands would be dangerous."

He smiled, pausing a few paces in front of Brak and the other man. A shudder of tension ran through Brak's gigantic body as Ankhma Ra subjected him to a moment's fierce scrutiny.

Would the man recognize the description of a barbarian hung up by his thumbs from a cypress? Surely Ankhma Ra had gotten such a description. Only the robes, the cloth-of-gold head wrappings might prevent such discovery. His fingers curled, ready to reach for the ornamental scimitar.

But apparently Ankhma Ra preferred to abuse someone less formidable looking. He glanced at the smaller man beside Brak. The wretch could hardly stand still, he was trembling so.

The iron gauntlets clanked as Ankhma Ra rolled the scarlet silk into a tiny ball. "The Silks of Shaitan (in the hands of a properly knowledgeable person, of course) have remarkable power. When they merely brush against human skin—

Suddenly Ankhma Ra threw the little ball of silk. It struck the retainer's bare throat. The man's eyes flew open. He arched his back and shrieked in agony.

Still balled, the silk clung to the man's skin like some supernatural leech. Where it touched, the man's flesh began to turn to dripping gray.

Ankhma Ra laughed again. He leaned forward, plucked back the silk, somehow swollen into a ball much larger than before.

The retainer shrieked again as the dripping grayness round his throat vanished. Moaning, he fell, kicked, and died.

Carefully, even daintily, Ankhma Ra peeled back the petaled corners of the silk.

Lord Tazim retched. Brak goggled, his belly cold. Even Princess Jardine pressed the back of her hand against her mouth and bit down.

Resting in the center of the silk in Ankhma Ra's hand was a pulsing, beating human heart, ripped bodily from the retainer's flesh by some demoniacal power. It was still bleeding. The heart's awful ooze seemed to blend into the curiously alive pattern of the silkstuff, blood upon blood.

Ankhma Ra turned. "Perhaps now, Lord Tazim, you comprehend why I require no great force of men. All I need do is offer my reluctant guests the gift of a silk." Then his lips writhed. From them came strange, cabalistic syllables Brak did not understand. The pulsing human heart began to change hue, darken.

On the face of Princess Jardine Brak now saw a wild, gruesomely fascinated little smile playing as the heart hardened, blackened, *hardened, blackened.*

With disdain, Ankhma Ra threw the petrified heart onto the pile of similarly frozen things beside the dais. As it struck, the heart clacked like a rock, dislodging several others. They rattled down the pile and rolled across the tiles.

"When the sun is up," Ankhma Ra said, "you will deliver the dowry chests." He replaced the silk and gauntlets and shut the cask. And, with a last quizzical glance at Jardine, he vanished through a hanging.

"Then, these many years… Lord Tazim looked suddenly much older, feebler. "The tales—all true. *Quickly,* out of this hellish place, both of you."

In the torchlit gloom of the apartments provided for them, Tazim and Brak held a whispered conference. The big barbarian, remembering the dead priest, his slaughtered pony, the slain retainer, said only: "I will try to kill him, Lord."

"By first light," Tazim shuddered, completely unnerved. "It must be by first light."

Grunting to conceal his own mounting dread, Brak swung round, knocked at the brass lock, opened the chest and dipped his powerful hands into opals and sapphires until his fingers touched the iron of his broadsword. He pulled it free and turned. The terrified Tazim had vanished. Brak was alone in the shadows.

Twice the silver grains within the hourglass, which Brak had found, trickled down before he set forth on his gory errand.

Emotion prodded him to start the moment he found himself deserted in the clustering blackness of this high, awful place. Instinct alone restrained him.

On the high steppes of his birth, the big barbarian had learned the primitive virtue of patience in stalking prey. Thus he paced the lavish apartment where the flung-open dowry chest threw back from jewel facets the flicker of low oil wicks. The night chill deepened. Again and again Brak glanced at the trickling silver grain.

When the last ones settled the second time, he gripped hard on the haft of his broadsword, blew out the last lamp and went stealing.

Here or there, a torch in a cresset illumined the distance. The opulent courts and halls remained empty as ever. Brak came to an intersection of corridors. He halted, puzzled. "Now," he muttered half aloud, "which way?"

His spine crawled as the echo of his voice came whispering back through the labyrinth: *Whichway—whichway—whichway—whichway…*

Mounting dread filled him. He tried to wipe from his mind the sight of that beating heart in Ankhma Ra's palm; wipe out the memory of the petrified heart tossed onto the pile that symbolized the sorcerer's truthfulness when he boasted that his demands were never rebuffed. Brak chose the right-turning of the cross corridor. From that direction a pearly light gleamed.

The broadsword haft in Brak's right hand grew slick with the dampness of chill fear. At least he was no longer encumbered by the so-called civilized garments, in which he felt less than free. The long, savage yellow braid hung down his brawny back where the lash marks stood out, barely healed. He was naked now save for the familiar garment of lion's hide about his hips.

Shortly he reached an arch that led into the pool court. The surface of the water was untroubled except by the light wind. The pool still radiated that eerie glow. The hundreds of petals bobbed like miniature fishing boats.

Long moments Brak crouched just within the arch, waiting and watching for sign of guards, of Ankhma Ra, or of the thing that supposedly swam in the bottomless pool. From his position, he could view a section of Ankhma Ra's apartments through an opening on the pool's far side. He saw the dais and a part of that monstrous rock pile half-veiled in gloom now.

A sound like muted laughter came drifting. Brak stiffened. He searched the court again... No one.

Perhaps it had been night birds crying out on the basalt peaks roundabout. Brak stole forward, intending to move around the left perimeter of the pool, enter Ankhma Ra's quarters, and then go past the hanging through which the wizard vanished. Brak would find him sleeping and drive the broadsword into his gut.

He was half the distance along the pool, moving like a ghost through the colonnade. Abruptly the sound came again. Even in this hour at the depth of the night, this hour of frozen stars, of loneliness and madness, he was sure. It was a woman's voice.

A whispering, bubbling turbulence disturbed the surface of the pool. Suddenly, above his head, iron squealed in the colonnade's roof. Brak whipped his head up as the hinges squealed louder.

Three brutes in corselets of hammered brass dropped through the trap one after another. They landed with thumps and curses. The first drove his long wickedly tipped spear at Brak's middle.

Brak leaped back, face contorted savagely as he hacked and parried. The broadsword's edge sliced into the soldier's arm at the elbow. Blood jetted. Brak lifted his foot, drove his naked heel against the brass breastplate.

The soldier stumbled backward. His spear fell out of his hand and rolled away, onto the pool's mosaic coping. With a ghastly cry the man splashed into the water. Blood from his wound spread out in a whirling cloud.

From somewhere in the depths of the pool there came new turbulence, as of something rising toward the spreading blood above.

The remaining pair of soldiers came on warily. They circled toward Brak from right to left. He crouched, mighty shoulders cording, tensed for the lunge he knew would come.

In his jumbled thoughts, one question thrust through: *How did they know I would be hunting for...?*

"At him," one of the soldiers snarled. Spear points out, both rushed.

Brak fastened his hands on the broadsword haft, brought it swinging from left to right in a huge chopping arc. His sudden high leap as he swung confused the soldier to his right. The man's spearhead tore only air as Brak came down again, hurling the man to the pavement.

The soldier writhed, tried to stab upward from a prone position with the spear. Brak rammed the broadsword point through the man's neck. Then the attacker on the left jabbed out with his spear.

A violent pain tore through the barbarian's right arm. He shouted in pain, tried to leap away, and tangled his feet on the other soldier's corpse.

Quick to press the advantage, the remaining soldier twisted his spear around. With two brutal smashes at Brak's forearm, he knocked the broadsword loose. The blade clanged and slid along the pool rim. Brak raised his hands to ward off the next blow. He was still off balance. Blood leaked down his right arm. The spear flew toward his face.

He twisted his head aside. The blow was telling anyhow, slamming him backward. By instinct alone did the barbarian manage to close his hands around the wood, trying to wrest the weapon away.

He moved too late. He was falling, his feet skidding and slipping.

Brak tumbled into the pool and sank like a stone through glowing water and bobbing petals.

Down and down into the pearl-shining depths he plummeted. At last his daze and numbness abated under the hurting of his lungs. He began to thrash upward again. A mammoth shadow flickered across his vision as he fought to the surface.

The spear was still clutched in his right hand. His head broke water. He panted for air. He saw that he had been carried to the center of the large pool.

Just as he tried to gather his wits and strength to pull toward the side, a series of iridescent spines, one behind the next, broke the surface not far away.

Treading water frantically, Brak saw the spines rise higher, higher still. Then utter horror filled him. He saw the ridged, green-slimed backbone to which the spines were attached.

Arrowing toward him came a thing of great slim-ness but immense length. It had a flat, milky-blind eye in either side of its head. The head looked malformed because it widened out twenty times the thickness of the creature's body and fanned, flicking tail. Gill slits as tall as Brak himself throbbed open and shut just above the water.

The immense round jaw of the gigantic fish opened, then opened wider still. From that maw gusted the stink of the wharf and charnel house.

Fangfish, Brak's brain screamed. He tried to swim away. But the weakness in his right arm and the weight of the spear dragged on him.

The tusks on the creature Ankhma Ra had bred and nurtured were unbelievably huge and white. The evil thing rapidly closed the distance to its newest meal.

Brak realized that the monster must be some vile crossbreeding of life forms older than time. It was able to lift its long fish's body half out of the pool by means of a series of froglike webbed appendages down either side of its shimmering scaled body. Brak counted twelve of those webbed half-legs on one side. They churned in a rhythm like galley oars as the Fangfish bore down.

Wider the stinking maw opened, lined with slimy, pink flesh. *Wider...*

As the monster mouth loomed, those immense ivory fangs had risen far above the surface; the jaw was full open. Pain and deathly fear beset Brak now.

He was too far from the pool's edge. The puny spear aching in his right fist would never penetrate the scales that glittered hard as armor.

Water roiled. Waves cascaded around him as the Fangfish hurled itself closer and closer, its maw gaping to swallow the bit of human meat bobbing before it.

He would die as best he could. Brak trod water ferociously and pulled back his throbbing right arm from which blood drained into the pearly water. He would launch the spear into the maw of the Fangfish, try to strike at the pulpy lining of...

Wildly Brak flailed. His back bumped against something afloat. He twisted his head. Spray flew in his face as the pool was thrashed into huge waves by the Fangfish almost upon him.

Drowned and bloated, hair floating weirdly, eyes open and swollen, it was the corpse of the first soldier with whom Brak had collided.

Mighty shoulders aching in torment, Brak floundered around and dove beneath the corpse. He drove the head of the spear upward under its chin, then thrust against the resistance of the water, which seemed heavy as lead. He shoved and thrust until the muscles in his brawny arms shuddered; at the last instant he let go.

Driven, with the dead man hanging on the spearhead like bait, the wooden weapon went into the maw of the Fangfish. Brak threw himself backward in the water as the huge milky eyes on either side of the fishhead brightened.

The corpse on the spear bumped the inside of the monster's maw. The fangs shut, snapping off the butt of the weapon. The closing of that awful mouth nearly swamped Brak in breaking waves. He was hurled violently against the pool side. He reached upward with his left hand to grasp and lift himself.

A black boot crushed down upon his left hand and pinned it.

Panting and almost blind, Brak flung his hand back. From the pool coping, Ankhma Ra was reaching down with an iron gauntlet.

"One way," came the voice through the ferocious ring in Brak's ears, "will do as well as the next—*assassin.*"

And while Brak hung by one hand on the pool rim, unable to let go, his mind paralyzed with surprise and fear, Ankhma Ra leaned down still further. He extended the ball of the Silk of Shaitan toward Brak's cheek.

Ankhma Ra's brittle laugh grew, a demoniac cackle racketing inside the walls of the barbarian's skull. Time seemed to stand still as that dreadfully alive bit of silk swelled and swelled in Brak's vision, drifting toward his skin to rip the heart from his chest by magic and petrify it.

A slash of iron blazed at the right corner of Brak's vision, reflecting torchlight from water droplets. It was his fallen broadsword.

Nearly blotting out the sight of that last hope, the Silk of Shaitan whispered and rustled toward Brak's face. The iron gauntlet grew larger, like the mailed fist of a gigantic statue.

With one pain-wracked lunge, Brak flung out his right arm. He slapped his hand down upon the broadsword haft. Then as the blood-hued silk seemed to fill all the world, Brak used the tip of the sword in his free hand to snag a corner of it and drive it back upward.

The first sound from Ankhma Ra was a startled gasp. The pressure on Brak's left hand ceased. In a wild scramble he flung himself up out of the pool.

The broadsword point had driven into the sorcerer's neck. Brak tottered forward and seized the haft. A burning, inhuman pain vibrated through his whole body, making him arch his back and shriek aloud in torment. But he held fast, pulling. The broadsword came out.

The Silk of Shaitan remained embedded in the wound in Ankhma Ra's pasty skin.

The moment Brak had freed the weapon, the worst of the pain stopped. He stumbled, and fell off balance from the force of the pull. Ankhma Ra plucked madly at the silk against his throat, tearing it loose with his iron gauntlets. But the very flesh of his neck was already dripping gray.

For one ghastly instant, the conjurer stood rigid, staring down at his own heart lying blood red and pumping on the silk in his hand.

Savage fury upon him, Brak leaped. He struck with the haft of his weapon. The thrust drove Ankhma Ra's flaccid body forward. Brak had a brief, mad vision of the sorcerer's iron gauntlet closing down upon the beating heart in one awful constriction before Ankhma Ra's body (living or dead now, Brak did not know) tumbled forward and dropped into the pool.

The spines of the Fangfish broke water again. The monster came slicing through hundreds of flower petals for its new tidbit.

There was a scuffling of boots. Brak turned, an incredibly savage, gore-streaked figure, broadsword in his blood-bathed right hand, the lion's hide hanging sopped around his middle. Six of Ankhma Ra's soldiers had slipped into the court in the gloom. Brak took one halting step toward them, his head abuzz, the killing urge driving him on.

"Come," he croaked in a hoarse, broken voice. "Come, soldiers. There is no conjurer to protect you with hell's tricks." He made a gesture with his broadsword, as if by invitation.

The first soldier uttered a faint, guttural cry, flung away his spear and plunged off into the shadows.

The others followed. Six spears, crisscrossed like match-wood, lay abandoned after they had gone.

Trying to shake the daze from his head, Brak was unprepared for the sudden fresh rip of agony down his back. He cried out, caught himself on a colonnade pillar. Even before he pulled himself around, he knew who it would be. The attack had come from behind; from the direction of the apartments of Ankhma Ra.

Standing there with Brak's blood glistening on the tip of a tiny dagger, her nightdress disarrayed, her hair unbound, her cheeks flushed and her breath tainted with wine, was Princess Jardine.

"He was a man of great parts," she said in a whisper. Her eyes were drunkenly bright. "He was better by far than that cow to whom my father would have married me. And you slew him. You, a witless, moneyless brute."

"He was a thing of filth," Brak croaked.

"I would have stayed with him. There was treasure here. There were delights." The Princess swayed, her eyes glazing slightly. Her lips curled into a smile that sickened Brak, for in it lay a love of awful vileness. He had suspected it was there, lurking beneath her loveliness, but now he saw it unmasked.

Brak shook his yellow head. "I watched the sorcerer glance at you, there in his chamber the first time. And you returned it. As if you'd found the kind of man who suited your black soul's need for..." Brak stopped, eyes flaring. "It must have been you. You went to him. So that he had men waiting."

"Yes." Princess Jardine gave a contemptuous toss of her head. "I slipped off to his night chambers and told him you were to be the assassin for my father."

Brak shambled forward. He lifted the broadsword with his throbbing, blood-dripping right arm.

"I am going to kill you, girl. I am going to kill you so Lord Tazim will never know what you became in this place, with that abomination of a man. Your father said you, of all his daughters, were a plague to him, didn't he? Well, no more." Brak twitched the sword at the pool. Its surface was calm again, save for the faint ripples that bobbed the floating flowers. "I can feed you to that creature and tell your father that Ankhma Ra himself destroyed you."

The laugh from the girl's lips was shrill.

"But you will never do that, barbarian. You are a man of *honor*. Or what you consider honor, anyway."

"I will." Brak raised the broadsword high.

Her eyes sparkled up at him defiant, assured.

"No," she said.

The evil taint was on her. Her beauty was hollow, betrayed by the sickening, knowing smile upon her mouth. Brak knew what she was. He knew what she had become when that which was deep within her had responded to the attraction of the conjurer. He lifted the broadsword higher, temples hammering.

Down came the sword again.

He could not strike.

She laughed, a tinkling sound. She darted the little dagger teasingly at Brak's exposed chest, like a flickering serpent's tongue. "I have no such scruples," she said merrily, as the dagger's tip bit into his flesh.

There was a pulping thud. The pricking against Brak's chest stopped. Grasping at the wood shaft vibrating in the center of her breast, Princess Jardine tried to pluck it out, in vain.

She staggered away. She cried out in wild terror at the sudden emptiness beneath her. Down she plummeted. Brak watched, shuddering in revulsion.

After a heartbeat or so, the spines of the Fangfish broke water. The maw opened, then clamped shut. The glowing pool roiled and then grew calm again.

Slowly the barbarian looked around. Where there had been six spears cast away by the frightened guards. Brak now counted five. In the murky shadows where he had listened, Tazim, Lord of the Tilling, raised his palms to cover his face and turned away, that he might weep in private.

In the sharp air of dawn, Lord Tazim rode back downward toward his kingdom. With fresh poultices upon his wounds and straddling his sole reward, a pony taken from among those belonging to Ankhma Ra's fled soldiers, Brak went the opposite way, following the trail downward into Kopt, the trail that pointed somewhere between the sunrise and Khurdisan. He had said few words to Lord Tazim the rest of the night.

Nor had he mentioned the bargain, or the dowry chests.

The only reward Brak wanted to claim was a quick and merciful forgetting.

PART FOUR

GHOSTS OF STONE

When umber evening fades to night,
The lonely pilgrim, parched and sore,
May hap upon the awful sight
Of thousands locked in granite tight,
All doomed as they were doomed of yore
In Chambalor.

When morning tints the wasted plain,
The lonely pilgrim wakes, looks o'er
The ruins, presses on again,
For all the ghosts in stone remain,
Still damned as they were damned before
In Chambalor.

—*Rhodymandias*, Canto IV

W hen the big barbarian opened his eyes, he thought he had gone mad.

Moments passed while the wind keened. He fought back the blinding ache from a great red sun searing its light into his face. And only then did Brak recall that this was not madness. Rather, it was the product of madness, of the sand, and of the wind.

Was it a day ago? Or a century? Gradually the memories returned.

Brak had ridden down from the mountain pass into the land of Kopt, and thence southward. For the better part of several weeks he had loafed along through this pleasant kingdom and that. At length he reached a border marker, crossed it into land that gradually changed from arid foothills to sandy waste.

At an oasis where caravan trails to the south intersected, he had been warned that the shortest route to Khurdisan was not necessarily the safest. If he followed a direct but little-used caravan trail, he was told, he would find himself in a red-sand waste where the breath of the gods often blotted the skies and earth with impenetrable storm clouds of sand.

Brak had struck out on the lonely trail nevertheless. And then the storm had struck, a whistling, gritty fury out of the west. He lost the trail completely. Now the siege was over, and Brak woke from hours of slumber. He remembered collapsing with exhaustion just as the hot wind was beginning to blow itself out. At least he could be thankful that he was alive.

Blinking into the reddish sundown, Brak felt for his broadsword. He discovered it still hanging at his hip. He rolled over.

Trackless waste stretched away. The wind lifted the sand in isolated veils here and there. He saw his pony where it had fallen, jaws, eyes, and ears so coated and filled that they looked like parts of some grotesque sand sculpture. At the height of the storm, while the heavens blackened, the pony had broken its leg. The poor dying beast had saved Brak's life, offering him a shelter until the worst of the storm passed on.

Brak's tongue was parched. He crawled toward the animal. He laid his palm against the pony's flank, uttered a guttural word of sorrow. At least he had been spared slaying the strong little beast.

Squatting on his haunches, Brak considered his predicament. He was in utter isolation. He had no provender, no water, and no real knowledge of where he was, except that he was lost in the middle of a vast desert. The warnings of the hook-nosed loafers back at the oasis he recalled now with bitter clarity. Only men with the feel of sand in their bones, only nomads born to this part of the world, attempted to cross this desert. And even they crossed at a relatively safe corner of the waste.

The waste, said the men at the oasis, was fearful. Once it had bloomed green and fertile, ages ago. But now it was cursed, dry, and empty. And haunted.

Rising, stretching the ache from his mighty body, Brak shouted: "Hallo? Hallo?" *Hal-lo, hal-lo*, the emptiness thundered back. The wind piping carried the grace notes weirdly. *Lo-lo-lo-lo...*

Brak walked to the top of a dune, calf deep in sand. At the top he shouted again. This time, the cry had a different, distorted sound. A moment later he saw why. Something had interrupted the emptiness. He gaped in wonder.

"At the oasis," he muttered to himself, "they talked of this place, I remember. I thought they were ignorant sots mouthing cradle tales. It had a name, I recall."

Then, like a thousand great gongs, the word came into his head before the word touched his tongue.

Chambalor.

"What did they call it? Chambalor the City of Gold Chariots." Brak's face was pained. "Well, it's a fine burial place, anyway."

The scene before him was awesome. Nothing remained of the city of Chambalor except two rows of pillars stretching into the distance. All else had been covered by the blood-lighted sand. Yet in the reddening evening, those pillars were magnificent, awful, majestic in their size.

How wide the great avenue must have been. The rows of pillars stood fully a quarter of a league apart. He counted fifty in each row, converging into the blurred distance before he lost track. And each pillar looked to be a hundred times as thick as a man, and fifty times as high. Up they soared, into the red sky.

While the big barbarian could not make out precisely what was carven upon their stone surfaces, the dimly-seen decorations lent the pillars a curious, shifting look, as though the stones were subtly alive.

With a sense of crawling horror washing over him, Brak thought of the livid, living skin of the arch-enchanter Septegundus. There was a strange kinship, like an echo of music, between the face of the sorcerer whom Brak had defeated in the Ice-marches, and these mighty pillars that seemed to blur and swim with a strange life all their own.

Brak screwed up his courage and decided to take a closer look at the ruins of Chambalor. He lurched down the other side of the dune, kicking up sand spray as he went. His single long, yellow braid bobbed down his naked back, above the garment of lion's hide at his hips.

In the shadow of one of those awesome pillars Brak could find protection when the night wind sharpened. Already the sun was down between the mighty twin rows of towering stone. It would be deep night soon.

Some blue-veined basalt had been unearthed by the windstorm, Brak saw. The barbarian kicked at the rock as he went by. He had taken two more steps when ghastly, stinging pain seared his left leg.

Looking down, he froze. A black, obscenely hairy feeler was twisting round and round his thick, tanned leg.

Even as his fist closed over the haft of his huge broadsword, Brak screwed his head around. No basalt slab lay there. Rather, a great lumpish black thing with transparent veins in intricate tracery over its body. The thing came rousing up out of the sand where it had lain asleep.

Through the transparent surface veins, a milky blue fluid full of black motes pumped. Two pouches on the sides of the black monstrosity opened. Great, ghastly pupil-less white eyes stared at him. From under the central body more feelers began to uncoil and extend. One closed around Brak's free arm. The stinging doubled.

With a roar and stir of sand, the enormous spider-like horror lifted itself on spindly legs and trundled toward its new enemy. A mouth yawned suddenly, giving off a wild, rhythmic *clacka-clacka-clacka*.

Hackles on his neck crawling, Brak sliced at the feeler constricting his arm. The edge of his broadsword barely dented the pulpish surface. *Clacka-clacka-clacka* went the mouth. The thing had a good two-dozen legs for propulsion. And twice that many feelers, all waving and questing in the dark red air. It lumbered closer to its prey.

Brak sawed hard at the tentacles. His heart thudded in his gigantic body. Taking a firmer grip on the haft of his blade, he lifted the iron over his head, and brought it flashing down.

With a jerk and a lash, the feeler was cleft.

Its backlash struck Brak in the cheek. Drops of hot, sticky ichor dribbled down his chin. That ichor burned like a fire-heated iron. The pain was far worse than that from the tentacle coiled around his calf. With another great stroke, Brak sliced that tentacle in half.

The *clacka-clacka* from the creature's maw stopped. Its white eyes clouded to a dark pearl.

Then, with a feeble little *scree* of hurt and anguish, the monster, some preternatural thing whose fellows had long ago died off, turned and went scurrying up the side of the dune.

Although huge, it moved with surprising speed. The last Brak saw of it, its fearsome feelers waved against the dark sky like a nest of worms. Then the beast vanished down the other side.

Brak held his broadsword a moment longer. He feared the nightmare thing would return. He heard nothing except the wind. He rubbed at his cheek. It burned almost beyond bearing. With a moan, he dropped to his knees.

He picked up a handful of sand. He rubbed it cruelly hard across his flesh. Still the dreadful ichor-touch pained. Dizziness began to creep over him. Had the fluid somehow been absorbed into his body, bearing its poisons to the center of his being? The two great rows of pillars of Chambalor seemed to waver, sway. Suddenly Brak wrenched over on his back with an inhuman shriek of pain.

His heels began to kick furiously. He could not stop the hurting. It increased each second. As he writhed, he experienced the delusion of thinking he would be rescued. Black against a distant dune, he thought he saw the humped, long-necked silhouettes of a pair of nomad dromedaries. Did the desert bells around their necks tinkle in the distance?

Pain blotted out the hallucination. Side to side Brak rolled, everything dimming, swimming, until, with a last gasp of agony, he slid down into soothing dark.

"Newt's toe, Hemp vein. Powder of sapphire...hmm, yes. The pouch is full enough."

"This is vile business, Father. To plan to bargain, haggle, when he may be dying."

"No doubt of it, daughter, he is dying. But not so swiftly as to justify your shrill accusations and hand-writings. 'Twill be the fullness of the sun tomorrow at the earliest before the toxic strains blend together. Although the fluid of T'muk is fatal, 'tis also slow to work. Hmmm. I'd thought the caravan masters had driven off the last of those creatures years ago. But I suppose since no man dares to visit Chambalor nowa-days, some of the beasts still lie in their dune burrows. We only saw it from a distance, but I'm sure this hulking lout, whoever he may be, did not slay it. T'muk is still about. And wounded, 'tis even more ferocious."

Dimly Brak heard the conversation against a back-ground of whistling wind and the crackle of a fire. He opened his eyes to a slit. The darkness lightened hardly at all. Then a fire pattern appeared, blurred, sharpened. Against it, the speakers were visible; two figures in flowing cloaks, both small, one feminine.

A brass desert bell tinkled. One of the humped beasts, which Brak had not imagined after all, blew its lips noisily.

Suppressing a groan, Brak sat up. "This place on my jaw," he said thickly. "There is much pain."

The robed man stirred, walked around the fire. The first thing Brak saw was the glitter of a silvery half-moon dagger with a bossed handle. The dagger was gripped in thin, frail fingers.

The man was incredibly old, wrapped in grimy white linens. Under its hem pointed slippers curled up. Out of his head wrapping his face peered like a cage-imprisoned monkey's; thin-lipped, heavy-nosed, with thousands of wrinkles. His pale green eyes, however, were ageless in the firelight. And though he was indeed spindly, he seemed to possess an aura of strength.

The man stood warily a few paces from Brak. He said, "Much pain there will be. And death, too. Unless I apply a poultice. I am a man of many professions, outlander. Mendicant is one, Magian apprentice is another, herb doctor is a third. And bargainer," with a cackling laugh, the old man bared perfect, even white teeth, "that is my best profession."

Brak saw that the ancient with the merciless greenish eyes indeed carried a fat pouch at his belt cord. Upon his breast rested a gold mystic symbol, a radiant star fastened to a link chain.

The man continued: "I will be pleased to concoct the necessary poultice, provided you lend your back and your broadsword, if need be, to an effort upon which I'm engaged." His wrinkled hand, fingernails longer than a woman's, lifted. By the sickled light of a moon, Brak saw him point to the strange stone pillars of Chambalor marching into the desert dark. "Yonder."

"Who are you?" Brak snarled. "A robber captain?"

"Nay, outlander, a man of commerce," chuckled the other. "Zama Khan, by name."

"Your callousness disgusts me!" said the second person beside the fire.

Zama Khan whirled. "It was not required that you come on this journey, Dareet." Then, with a vicious crinkling of his mummy's lips, he bowed at the barbarian lying sprawled on the sand. "My daughter Dareet has been stricken by a peculiar malady, outlander. An attack of scruples."

Now full consciousness, and with it anger, returned to the yellow-haired barbarian. Before he could speak, however, the girl Dareet rushed forward. She confronted her father:

"Long and long have I followed you from one dishonest living to another, hoping to change you, hoping to soften you, and only watching you grow harder, more avaricious. But this last is too much. It was not enough that you drugged the wine of that merchant of Vishnuzin, then fled the city with those gimcrack clay tablets. Now your lust for a treasure that doesn't exist has maddened you to the point where you'll make an innocent man join in your madness or pay with his life."

"Those silver doors are mouldered with age," Zama Khan said. "We cannot open them alone."

"So this poor stranger, dying from the kiss of T'muk, must help, or you'll not help him?"

From deep in his throat Brak growled, "You are saying many things that are strange to me. Who are you? What kind of treasure are you hunting? And what is T'muk?"

Licking his lips, Zama Khan hunkered down. He still gripped the dagger. "T'muk is the ancient name for the primitive sand spider that attacked you. The caravan masters know him as The Thing Which Crawls. That specimen you hacked is lurking about. 'Tis another reason for us to be away before the moon fully wanes."

Zama Khan ran his thumb along the dagger's shining edge. Beyond the crouching man, Brak saw the face of the girl Dareet illuminated by the dung-chip fire. A thin, rather undernourished face. She was Sloe-eyed, olive skinned, and pretty, too, except for the gloss of fear on her face. The girl sensed evil in the empty desert night. An evil larger than that in the green, heartless eyes watching Brak where he lay. What was that evil? Brak wondered.

Trying to quell his anger, Brak thought perhaps he might reason with this strange old man. He said,

"While passing through your land, I've heard of this place, Chambalor. What is it you seek here?"

"First," came Zama Khan's prompt reply, "why is it that you pass through at all?"

"My name is Brak. I come from the high steppes, and I'm traveling to Khurdisan in the south."

Zama Khan snorted. "A barbarian! With no skill in letters or numbers or the magic arts. Well, stranger Brak, that matters little, I suppose. Your back is wide and roped with muscle. Pitting that back against the silver doors to the treasure chamber, you should be able to open them. Then, with the tablets that I—ah—released from the possession of the merchant in Vishnuzin, I shall read the incantation, clearly written. I shall shatter the wizard's spell upon the ivory chest, which is sealed to a block of marble, so the tablets say. If it were not so sealed, I'd carry it off entire. The contents will go into the camel bags, and one night's work shall make up for a life of poverty, of crawling and scraping before the nabobs."

Dareet said softly, "Never until now, Father, did I see you in true light. There is a twisted evil in you which nothing can untangle now."

"Be silent!" Zama Khan cried. "You're flesh of my loins, but you sicken me."

"No more than I am sickened by seeing you at last for what you are."

Once more Brak's cheek began to burn and tingle. The pain nearly doubled him. He gasped out: "You're— not lying to me? There are—are medicaments in your pouch to—fix a poultice so the—monster's touch won't—be fatal?"

"That is so," answered Zama Khan. "In return, you will come with my daughter and me into the ruins. Help us force the doors."

With a small sound of disgust, Dareet turned away. Brak waited a moment longer. He wondered whether he was being skillfully gulled. Suddenly his anger flamed. He whipped his hand across, wrapped his fingers around the broadsword haft.

Breast chain clanking, Zama Khan was swifter. He leaped. The dagger flashed. Zama Khan crouched suddenly beside Brak, the flat of the blade bearing down cruelly on the barbarian's wrist, bending it enough so that it was pinned, and he could not draw the broadsword swiftly.

Though Zama Khan's teeth were perfect white, foul breath gusted from his mouth as he whispered: "Bare your iron and you'll not live another sundown, outlander. I promise."

Brak looked at Dareet. She nodded. "He speaks truth. Though you might take the pouch from him by force, you could not mix the poultice. Nor could I."

T'muk, Brak thought. *The Thing Which Crawls.* Its poison stung his flesh, hurting, *hurting...*

"Very well," he said low. "I will try to open your silver doors. But fix the medicine first, and apply it."

Chuckling, Zama Khan stood up. He sheathed his dagger with a click. "Why, yes, friend Brak. That I will do. I have you at a disadvantage, you see. I can tell you give a promise that is kept. I know you will do what you say. While I..." Zama Khan shrugged, "...well, you must trust in me."

He lifted the flap of his pouch, took out a stone mortar, a smaller stone chipped into a rod shape, and several phiales. Brak watched, simmering with fury. Zama Khan had rightly seen that, once making a bargain, Brak would stand by it. So he was immediately at a disadvantage.

Devious and wicked were the ways of the world through which he traveled to seek his fortune. The only boon Brak's agreement had gained him was a kind of sad and thankful look of relief from Dareet. She sat across the fire, starting and shivering with each whine and gust of wind.

Presently Zama Khan daubed a sticky yellowish mess upon Brak's jaw. He pressed several dry leaves against it. "Hold those in place a moment or two. 'Twill work rapidly."

That part was true, anyway. The pain soon lessened. As Zama Khan handed Brak a scrap of gray linen with which to wipe his cheek, the latter asked, "What is it you seek in Chambalor, old man? You spoke of a treasure. Surely none exists. Though I'm an outlander, I heard the tales back at the way stations. Chambalor flourished generations ago, in a time almost beyond memory."

Zama Khan's greenish eyes showed pinprick reflections of the firelight. "Aye. But consider those stone pillars. Have you looked at them closely?"

"No. I got no nearer than the den of T'muk."

"Then give a glance when we reach them. For on, or perhaps in those pillars, frozen in damned torment, sealed in stone to live their agonies forever, are the princes and courtesans of Chambalor. The warlords and the women who once in a dim time made Chambalor the feared and savage kingdom she was."

Almost crooning, Zama Khan began to rock back and forth on his heels. His eyes stared off toward the obelisks rising in the moon's glare.

"She was a sink. A pit of cruelty, war, and bestial evil, was Chambalor. One man, one powerful leader drove the people down to these depths of lust and depravity."

"The king?" Brak asked, low voiced.

"No, a wizard. A wizard called Septegundus."

The name rang in Brak's mind again like a sonorous, sinister bell. *Generations ago? How could that be?*

The answer came back, *Because Septegundus never dies, only walks the world at will, to bring it evil.*

"The Lord of Chambalor," Zama Khan crooned on, "grew tired of this fomentation of evil and drove a knife into the sorcerer's heart. No blood poured forth upon the ground, so says the tale. And evil smokes and fumes arose from the place where Septegundus stood. The wind smote Chambalor in a maelstrom, and before Septegundus vanished in the smoke he cursed Chambalor. His spell locked Chambalor's treasure—emeralds, piles and piles of emeralds from the mines that once flourished nearby—in an ivory chest behind silver doors.

"And to revenge himself upon the Lord, the wizard froze all the people of Chambalor in rock, even those who had followed him. Thousands of them he locked in each of the great columns along the triumphal avenue, and it all happened in a breath's time. Before the smoke rose, the wizard had vanished.

"In later times, a certain wandering mendicant—called Juhad, he was, Juhad the Pit-walker—claimed to have had concourse with this master-sorcerer Septegundus. Juhad carried with him until the day he died tablets of clay, written upon with a stylus. Those tablets bore the incantation that would release the tormented souls of Chambalor and, incidentally, the treasure one day.

"Juhad defended the tablets from many a thief, saying that his master, Septegundus, to whom he'd been 'prenticed in his youth, would decide when Chambalor had suffered enough. Juhad vanished in a sandstorm of the kind that swallowed you up, barbarian. But his clay tablets endured, passed from hand to frightened hand, age upon age. I—ah—borrowed them, as I mentioned, from the merchant I chanced upon in Vishnuzin."

The big barbarian could not resist a snort of disbelief. "Old man, 'tis a fable."

Dareet gave a shudder. "You are wrong, barbarian. No one has plundered the treasure precisely because it is real. Many times, they say, others have wanted to come. Some, the awful T'muk has frightened away. Others—well, Chambalor is cursed. Not until this twisted soul who once was my father was there a man greedy enough, or mad enough, to dare at last…

With a cry, Zama Khan struck her. Brak leaped to his feet, pulled the broadsword. Zama Khan's half-moon dagger whispered out, winked in the moon.

"I think not," he said. His evil monkeylike face smiled. "A bargain is a bargain."

"Then let's be done!" Brak grumbled.

He was convinced the old man had lost his wits. Despite encountering Septegundus before, Brak felt sure nothing remained of Chambalor's fabled wealth except a lustful dream passed from generation to generation. But when Dareet began to weep, Brak had doubts.

Brak put his arm around the girl's shoulder. After making a sneering remark about the barbarian's solicitude, Zama Khan moved off into the dark, where a dromedary stamped.

Standing with his arm around the shaking girl, Brak realized that for the first time in his life, he actually had the desire to break his word. He wanted to go so far as to gut Zama Khan with his broadsword, from behind. The only reason that he did not was Dareet.

She was shaking violently now. She was a frail girl. He did not want to leave her alone with the green-eyed old madman, who now came back into the firelight clutching a bundle wrapped in frowsy lambskin.

Zama Khan's brown fingers trembled as he unwrapped the bundle. "These are Juhad's tablets," he breathed, his face lightly slicked with sweat, his lower lip trembling with expectation. "Let us put them to use. Bring your broadsword, barbarian. And the girl, if she can walk. Or, if she chooses, she can remain here."

"No!" The outcry from Dareet was sharp. "This place is accursed."

Three shadows, they set out across the dunes and soon reached the head of the buried avenue.

The mammoth pillars towered up on either hand, black against the moon and casting blacker shadows. Brak's stomach turned over and sour bile rose in his mouth as he studied the carvings reaching to the sky.

Round and round each pillar, in endless circling friezes, the princes of Chambalor and their begirdled women were portrayed with such vividness that Brak felt thousands of damned, tormented eyes watching him.

The garments, and the appointments surrounding the figures, were splendid indeed, though they had an ancient look. But the figures themselves...

Sickened, Brak turned away from one lower band on the first great pillar. Upon it, stone soldiers in breastplates bashed out the heads of babes by holding their ankles and swinging them. Murder, plunder, torture, lust, depravity; no vice was missing, no sin unrepresented, as figure after figure, group after group, had been caught by Juhad's curse. So many sins actually defied belief. Though he had seen much of savagery, in just a moment or so, Brak viewed many things of which even he had never dreamed.

The most hideous feature of all was the look upon each of the faces. Over his shoulder as he walked, Brak could see many in the moon glare. And each face showed *torment*.

He'd seen such torment before, on the crawling skin of the Amyr of Evil upon Earth.

They kept trudging.

"Yonder," Zama Khan said at last, rushing ahead. Brak had already counted fifty-five pillars on his left. Now he glimpsed at least a dozen more ahead. "The last on the left was the treasure tower," Zama Khan called. "Below ground lies the chamber."

Suddenly Brak stopped. Dareet gripped his arm. "What do you hear, barbarian?"

"Fancies," Brak whispered in reply. He scanned the dune horizon, black, silver bathed, empty beyond the pillars. Had the wind carried a faint *clacka-clacka-clacka*?

No, he was dreaming.

As they approached the final pillar on the left, Brak saw a dark opening in the base. Outside of this, Zama Khan waited, hands clutching tightly at the bundle. The clay tablets shone dull gray where the wrappings fell away. Stark black lines upon them were the places where a stylus had inscribed many strange, ancient symbols before the tablets hardened. All at once, Brak began to believe...

Zama Khan was mad in his own way. But the story of Chambalor's curse might be true... Impossible!

Then why did Brak have the uneasy feeling that beneath the stone surfaces of the carved depravities rising on every hand, a tormented, imprisoned life crawled and writhed, awaiting release?

"There's tinder inside," Zama Khan whispered. "I'll strike a spark."

In a moment, he had a smoky torch going. There was a smell of decay, dust, as they hurried down a winding stair. They emerged into a wide, paved circular hall. At the far side, huge silver doors, greenish-blue with mold growths in their crevices, shone dully.

"The right hand one gives but a little." Zama Khan's voice was hushed, echoing. "The left not at all."

"This is wrong." Dareet was trembling. "This is wrong. And too dangerous. Father," she seized the old man's arm, *"why else has no one ever come before us? Because they knew...*

"I will not be balked!" Zama Khan screamed, slashing at her with his hand. The sound of the blow was loud, sharp. Dareet fell, sobbing.

Watching Zama Khan, Brak let his thick yellow brows hook together in a ferocious scowl. The old man licked his lips.

"The bargain," he said softly, his green eyes bright. "The bargain is to open the doors."

Turning, Brak pushed his shoulder against the right-hand door of silver. It squealed faintly, moved hardly at all.

He braced his palms against the door, pushed harder. The muscles in his mighty shoulders and brawny arms corded, pulsed, jumped. His hands grew damp with sweat. He had to stop and wipe them on the garment of lion's-hide at his waist.

He pushed harder, still harder. His forehead began to hurt. The door opened a hand's width, then two.

Foul fetid air gushed out. Zama Khan's breathing was dry, intense behind him. Brak pushed with all his might. His belly muscles corded. His thews strained. Three hand's widths... Four.

"A little more!" Zama Khan cried, straining forward with the torch. "A little more and the bargain is accomplished."

Brak threw his whole body against the door, felt it sway, give a squeal of tortured fittings, lurch inward. Simultaneously, Dareet's scream rose up:

"Brak!"

Long yellow braid swinging, the gigantic barbarian spun. Zama Khan had thrust the torch into a rusty iron wall bracket. The half-moon dagger blazed, arcing higher, higher, as Zama Khan's robes flowed out behind him, driven by the rush of his charge.

"I've kept my word," he was babbling, his white teeth ashine with spittle. "The bargain is ended and only I will go through the doors to the ivory chest of…"

The whirling broadsword blade in Brak's two hands cut off Zama Khan's words in a shower of blood, and cut off half his head, too.

For one insane instant, Brak saw the corpse still alive. It wobbled before him on its curl-toed slippers, the light of treachery dying in its green eyes as its head hung half-severed on its neck. Then Zama Khan's robes were showered with the blood that fountained up and out of his neck. His hands opened and he dropped the half-moon dagger and the tablets of Juhad.

The clay tablets smashed apart.

The light that followed the clap of noise when the tablets broke was white as lightning, searing-white. Brak was hurled back against the wall. Dareet shrieked wildly. Beyond the silver door standing half open, that blazing brilliance bloomed. An ivory chest that had been fused upon a stone block became a billow of smoking thunder.

Green flowers grew in the radiance, then crumbled and fell apart in midair, dripping down like green rain. Shaking with terror, Brak stumbled across the antechamber. The very foundations of the great pillar began to rock. The very air seemed to swirl and darken with a rush of wind.

Then, from somewhere, a ghastly screaming chorus of thousands upon thousands of cursed, condemned souls began to wail and howl.

"The place will collapse," Brak yelled, seizing Dareet's thin arm, dragging her along toward the stairs, pulling her upward. "The shattered tablets broke the curse. But they must have broken something more, because…"

Milk white and round, great eyes stared at Brak from the head of the stairs.

Beneath the surfaces of the transparent veins twisting obscenely over the humped body of T'muk, pale blue liquids flowed and pulsed. *Clacka-clacka-clacka* went the mouth. Two of its feelers dangling useless, The Thing Which Crawls came limping downward toward the enemy who had hurt it.

"Back, girl!" the big barbarian cried. "Hide at the bottom."

"The pillar is shaking, the earth is trembling," Dareet moaned.

"Go!" Brak bawled. "There is no other way out of..."

Clacka-clacka-clacka. The Thing Which Crawls came down and around on the stairs, its vile body jammed between the walls, its feelers waving. Brak charged up half-a-dozen steps, raised the broadsword over his head. Then cold pit-terror claimed him.

Bring the blade down upon a feeler, cut one of the thing's evil, worm-like, lashing arms, and the ichor would flood again.

Zama Khan was dead.

And only Zama Khan knew how to mix the healing poultice.

Brak was wracked with the agony of uncertainty.

Clacka-clacka-clacka.

From out of time, from a forgotten world, T'muk came squeezing and oozing and crawling down the stairs while Brak retreated a step, another, shaking with weariness and desperation.

If he died, the girl Dareet would die as well.

He reached the bottom of the stair again. The base of the pillar rocked. The awful chanting, moaning, had intensified now. It sounded from above ground.

There was one chance. One chance, and he must gamble it. Brak could use the weapon only this way.

He closed his right hand midway along the cruelly sharp sword blade. Closed his fingers and bit his lips until blood ran because the sword edge sliced so deep. But he could get a grip no other way.

Then, drawing back his right arm, he threw the sword, spear fashion, feeling his own bloodied palm slide away as the iron sailed straight and hard. It was buried haft deep in the right eye of The Thing Which Crawls.

Clacka-clacka-clacka, clacka-clacka-clacka... The mouth pulsed frantically. The hairy crawling legs twitched. Brak stumbled down to where Dareet crouched. He shielded her with his own sweat-streaked body. His right hand was running raw with gore as T'muk the ancient thrashed and heaved and died, jammed into the stair.

Brak whispered shakily, "Now—we must climb up and over. There is only a little ichor leaking from the eye. We can pass it safely."

But as they climbed the stair, the stench of the dead creature reached them. Dareet gave a long, struggling cry and went limp. Brak slung her over his shoulder.

He tried to keep his mind clear to concentrate on what he was doing. He planted a foot on the hideous, black-haired hump of the dead monster. Gripping other tufts, he began to climb.

Once he slipped.

Sobbing, he hung on, his foot shaking and trembling, just the width of a finger from slipping into the gleaming ichor track that leaked down out of the skewered eye.

Slowly, with all the strength in his mighty body, he controlled that one trembling leg, pulling it up and away. Leaving the broadsword where it was, he kept climbing.

Outside, there was maelstrom.

The wind had risen. Great dark clouds of sand whipped past in the night, stinging his face. Brak tried to walk. His body was pushed into an oblique angle by the force of the storm. He somehow knew that was not like the storm that had felled him earlier. The winds blew black, palpable, whirling round and round each of the great pillars, then rising up toward the sky in train after train of writhing lifelike stuff. Within these clouds, awful human shapes twisted, turned, moaned, moaned, *moaned*...

Carrying Dareet in his arms, Brak the barbarian staggered as far as the end of the avenue before the wind and the blinding sand and the awful ascending moans weakened his body and mind and hurled him senseless to the earth.

At dawn, his hacked hand bound in linen, Brak ventured once more into the treasure-house pillar to fetch the body of Zama Khan.

Peering into the treasure room, he saw nothing except bare, mouldering black walls. In the center of the floor, a scattering of ivory chips lay among green emerald dust. The treasure was no more.

Returning to the campsite, he helped Dareet bury the old man. Because she professed no religion, he thought of Friar Jerome's Nameless God. Brak fashioned a crude cross of Nestoriamus from bits of a stick and placed it in the blowing sand over the mound. Perhaps it would help.

Dareet stood with her head down. Brak wiped his mouth. He was heavy with guilt.

"My sword killed him," he grumbled. "I—I am sorry."

"It makes no difference." The girl's voice was empty. "We must leave."

"The beasts will carry us." Brak was still tortured. "Girl, I had to kill him."

"It makes no difference," she repeated. "He was evil. The greed that drove him to come here, where no sane man would come, made him a stranger to me long ago. He was not my father." But despite her words, she began to weep, shuddering in her sorrow.

At length Brak put his arm around her. "Girl? It has just come to me. The dark gods have strange ways. Your father came here to plunder. Yet the breaking of the tablets released thousands of tormented sufferers from the prison where the wizard's spell cast them. Though he never intended it, your father freed them from their pain and ended their bondage. Surely, surely that is something for which to honor him. All men must be honored in some way."

The wind whistled, keened in the silence.

"Dareet? I speak the truth. You can see it. Look. You must look."

She did, seeing for perhaps the first time that the mighty pillars of Chambalor, standing in the blinding white desert sun, were bare. Bare of ornament, the figures—gone.

Slowly Dareet's eyes cleared. Wearily she lifted one hand. "Yes. I see. He freed them. It is something. We, we must see to the beasts."

In an hour, Brak and the girl and the dromedaries were gone beyond the horizon.

PART FIVE

The Barge of Souls

Down from the north rode a wild barbarian,
Down from the north with his sword in his hand.
Down from the north rode Brak the barbarian,
Seeking the way to a far-distant land.

Bound for the south and the warm climes of Khurdisan,
Bound for the south where the gold idols gleam.
Bound for the south rode Brak the barbarian,
Seeking the way to a golden dream.

Black was the pain of the wild barbarian,
Black was the pain for the maid on the hill.
Black was the pain of Brak the barbarian.
He rode away and he rides somewhere still.

—Tyresias, *The Song of Brak*

Further down the bed of the dry water course the big barbarian had been following, the trail twisted around and out of sight past an up-thrust pillar of obsidian. It was from around this bend that the terrified shriek came keening.

Brak had been sitting on his haunches on one sloped side of the water course while his pony rested. Now he rose. The normal tightness of his belly increased as his mind absorbed the wail of terror, together with the eerie sound that followed it a moment later.

The sound was something like a prolonged, dryish rasp, as of a rough, calloused warrior's palm being scraped over rock. The resemblance ended there. The sound was so loud that, to make it, the warrior would have needed to own a hand fully as wide as Brak himself was tall. And that was tall indeed.

Scrape-and-grind. That was the noise, repeated with a sinister persistence.

Brak hesitated. He did not relish mingling in affairs that were none of his concern. Another moan, unmistakably human, followed a brief pause in the scraping. The moan obviously came from the throat of the same man who had shrieked in sudden alarm a moment before.

Brak scrambled down the slope and slapped his pony's lathered neck.

"Enough rest, now." He swung up. "We'll see what grinds away the rock yonder, and who's so afraid of it."

Gently the big barbarian kneed his pony along. He reached across his waist to free the haft of the mighty broadsword bobbing in its immense scabbard. The hour was twilight.

The country through which Brak had been traveling for the past six days was a jumble of blasted, multicolored rock. The land looked like the result of an evil god reaching down with a fist, smashing one great stone and breaking it into score upon score of random parts, some the size of boulders, some the size of small mountains, but all predominantly glassy-black. Save for distant gleams from war chariots traveling the opposite way from that which he was taking (Brak was bound roughly south), he had seen no sign of human life in all his six days in the wasteland.

The flesh on his bare back prickled as he neared the watercourse bending. He shushed his pony. He tugged its milky mane to slow its pace to a soft-hoofed clop. Two sounds became clearly defined.

First, the human (in pain or fear or both) had begun a low, continuous cry, wordless except for an occasional babbled syllable that might have been an appeal for help. Then, against this, like a hideous counterpoint, came that huge, ominous *scrape-and-grind* of something dragging down over rock surfaces.

"Whatever thing makes that racket," Brak breathed to himself, "'tis not small."

Just this side of the obsidian pillar, Brak halted his pony. He slid the broadsword loose with an iron whisper. The brooding, diffused light of red sunset was falling from his right. Across the jumbled southern horizon, great palls of inky smoke blew. The smoke was closer now than it had been when the barbarian first sighted it just this past dawn.

War smoke? It seemed logical, judging from his glimpses of wheeling chariots hammering north.

In retreat? Yes, if their speed meant anything.

Brak had no notion who the combatants might be. He was a stranger, in a strange kingdom.

The voice ahead rose, clear with hysteria: "The Horned Lady protect me! The Horned Lady accept my soul and carry it beyond the Dark Veils to paradise. May I dwell in paradise numberless days! May my soul know peace, absolution, comfort in the Horned Lady's embrace."

Digging in his bare heels, Brak headed the pony forward in a trot. The man was crying a prayer, and it sounded like the prayer of one with not much time left to live.

"The Horned Lady bless me with her eternal embrace," came the terrorized voice as Brak burst around the outcrop, riding hard.

Light and shadow interplayed where the watercourse widened. As Brak hurled himself from his pony's back, he had time enough for a quick estimate of what had happened.

A huge-wheeled bronze chariot had overturned, throwing its driver from the car. From the rolled upper rim of the car, wicked knife blades protruded, short and glittering, spaced about three fingers apart. The charioteer had been gored by two of these spiny daggers, which were obviously meant to fend off those who would leap aboard the chariot to attack. The driver lay beneath the car, an indistinct blur of bronze armor and creeping redness.

Brak's rapid impression convinced him that here was a different kind of chariot from those he had distantly observed rolling away to the north. Upon the front of this car, in rich bronzed bas-relief, was the device of a goddess.

She was a comely young woman, shown from the waist upward, and without garment or ornament, except for a thin dagger hanging down upon a linked chain between her breasts. From her bronze forehead sprouted two horns of lovely whorled intricacy. In one of her uplifted hands she held a sheaf of plenty. In the other she tore a lightning fork down from the sky.

The Horned Lady. The image of the warrior-goddess was picked out by a beam of red light that fell aslant the car. Her bronzed eyes seemed to mock Brak, defy and dare him.

All these details the big barbarian absorbed almost in a breath's time. Abruptly he heard again the scrape-and-grind, so loud this time that it hurt his ears.

Brak whipped his head around. Up the slope, he saw what made the noise, and choked. Six times longer than Brak was tall, the slug-like creature was like some great tube of sinuous substance. Far overhead, the black mouth of its burrow in the obsidian mountain stood out. From this the creature must have been roused.

All along its cylindrical body it had small, white, pulpy appendages, the merest vestiges of legs. It actually seemed to propel itself down the slope and around boulders toward the dying charioteer by means of an obscene wriggling action. Rather than by skin, it was protected by lizard-shiny plates which gleamed with a gray-metal luster. These plates were hinged together by moist pink membranes Brak could glimpse as the body articulated. The plates scraping rock caused the grinding sound.

And as the monstrous thing worked its way down toward its victim under the chariot, that armor-plated body smashed and ground the solid rock beneath it to dust.

Armor that could pulverize obsidian? Brak's brain nearly boggled. But the frightful cloud of dust hanging in the air behind the crawling nightmare testified to the abrasive strength of those plates.

At the head of the tubelike thing, two round, opalescent eyes twice as large as Brak's own head burned in the gloom. The thing was drawing near the flat bottom of the watercourse. Half of its body still extended up the slope. Suddenly a slit in the lower part of its head opened.

Tensely crouched, broadsword bared, Brak waited with the blood-hammer of danger running high in his veins. All pretense that he might be civilized had vanished from his face, which was ugly. Twilight scarlet glinted on his blade. He was a savage figure, a brawny animal like the very beasts he had hunted in the wild lands of the north that gave him birth.

The charioteer continued to babble his delirious prayer. Slowly, slowly, a moist, evil, sickeningly red tongue began to uncoil from within the beast's slit-like mouth. On the surface of this long tongue, tiny sucking polyps waved to and fro.

The creature gave a frantic wrench to the rear part of its body and advanced again, up and over a small boulder. There was a grind and screech of abraded rock. The boulder collapsed into whorled dust.

The long tongue uncoiled and uncoiled, slithering across the bed of the watercourse as though it possessed life of its own. Then, almost as if the creature sensed Brak's presence, the tongue turned toward him suddenly.

The vile sucking polyps waved with even greater agitation. All at once, however, the tongue retracted.

A moment later it slid out along its original course.

The charioteer had pushed himself up on his palms. He watched the scene with horror-crazed eyes. Below the waist his body was hidden by the deadly tines of the chariot. He stifled another scream as the tongue started toward him and the lizard-armor body followed, crushing and pulverizing rock as it moved.

Brak wrenched himself free of his state of dazed awe.

Swiftly he hauled up a smooth, oval rock with his free hand. He felt his back thews wrench as he shot his arm forward to hurl the rock through the air. His aim was true. The rock smashed down upon the fantastically long, creeping tongue.

Vile ichor squirted suddenly from the crushed polyps. The creature's tail region thrashed. Two gigantic boulders were blasted to a hail of pumice. Bits of the sharp, stinging rock rained down upon the yellow-haired barbarian.

Now the opalescent eyes rolled in Brak's direction again. But there was a bloody smell suffusing the air around the chariot, and Brak sensed that the monster could somehow scent the warm stuff. The creature sent its tongue shooting out again, straight toward the pinned charioteer.

Instantly Brak knew what he must do. He covered the ground in long strides, ramming the broadsword back in its scabbard as he bawled, "Cover your head! Hide your face and pray that those iron teeth miss you this time!"

Then he was leaping across the ripped ends of the traces, from which the chariot horses must have bolted loose, and he was around to the car's other side. Rapidly he calculated angles. He hoped the car would fall far enough. He brushed past the wheel which was upturned to the twilight sky and set it spinning as he thrust his shoulder against the car's bottom. He pushed hard.

A savage, angry grunt of effort slipped from his lips.

The bronze car was fiendishly heavy. Worse, the charioteer had begun to babble again. Perhaps out of fear that he would be crushed, but more probably, Brak guessed, because that polyp-quivering tongue would be near him now, ready to—what? Suck the flesh from his bones?

Brak strained and shoved. His back began to ache violently. His left foot slipped. A point of rock slashed it bloody as he fought for balance.

The chariot lurched a little.

He had to move it. He had to tip it. His forehead throbbed as he pushed harder and still harder.

And, so close that it seemed to drown out all other sounds in the universe, the evil *scrape-and-grind* signaled that the rock-creature was drawing closer to its quarry.

Brak bent his whole body into the effort to overturn the car. His head beat and sang. Suddenly the car gave a distinct, sharp lurch.

But still it did not fall.

The charioteer let out the most hideous scream Brak had ever heard from a human throat. The big barbarian knew the monster's polyp tongue had touched the man's flesh. With a shout of primitive rage, Brak slammed his whole gigantic body against the car a last time. The jolt nearly knocked him senseless. But the car began to tip.

It seemed to hesitate, hanging balanced. Then it toppled.

Brak leaped back. The charioteer writhed as one of the knives embedded in the car's rim raked the flesh of his thigh. Crashing, the chariot fell.

And a whole long row of those same rim knives slashed down through the polyp tongue, piercing it, pinning it to the earth of the watercourse.

The monster's lizard-plate tail began to whip back and forth through the air, shattering any rock it touched. One huge fragment struck Brak on the forehead as he fastened a hand on the car's wheel. He leaped up on the precariously teetering vehicle.

The monster was trying to pull its pierced tongue free, and its efforts sent a series of sickening jolts through the car. Brak braced his bare soles around one edge of the chariot's car.

Then he leaned out. He hung from the wheel by his left hand, straining down, down *down*, and drove his broadsword into the monster's opalescent right eye.

Like a madman he struck again, again, thrust after thrust, until the eyes were lightless, blood-boiling pods. Then he let go and jumped wide. He landed on his chest, the wind knocked out of him.

The rock-monster gave one last thrash. This deathly quiver seemed to shake the earth's foundations. Then, as pumice and dust drifted down and settled, the thing died.

Panting, Brak picked himself up. He cleaned his broadsword blade in the dirt and sheathed it. He staggered to where the charioteer lay. The whites of the man's eyes shone faintly in the gloom. The sun had set. Only a few faint beams of redness isolated points along the watercourse. Brak and the charioteer were shrouded in dark.

The big barbarian knelt over the dying man.

The man gasped, "The Horned Lady—will not—receive me in shame now."

"You could not fight the thing," Brak said. "The knives gored you."

"The Horned Lady—expects—a death of honor. At least when the chariot overturned—I was—pursuing our enemies."

"There was a battle," Brak stated. "The sky hangs with smoke."

"Aye, a battle." The man's breath whistled reedily between his teeth. "We—the Horned Lady's people—the people of Phrixos the Shining River-—we turned back the armies of the hairy men of Gat. We fought there, that way."

One gauntleted hand twitched out, indicating south. The charioteer panted on: "Long have the men of Gat threatened us. Phrixos is—the delta of the Shining River, a narrow, fertile land along—both its shores. We defended our land. We sent the hairy men of Gat away with but a tenth of the numbers which they had when they—rode to attack us. But we paid a price. Many of us paid—a price."

Abruptly the charioteer began to cough. Brak gnawed his lip.

"Where are the physicians with your army?" he asked.

"Gone," was the reply. "Back to the cities by the Shining River. I was sent out after the Gat stragglers. The chariot overturned—my own chariot knives cut me to death. In the dust, the noise—my comrades did not see the accident, and— raced on. My own knives." He coughed hard. "A bad joke, eh? A physician won't help. But you have helped, stranger. To die unable to fight that foul thing would—be dishonorable. The rock beasts have lived in these hills since before time itself. And to die without fighting—the Horned Lady would know. She might not fetch me down the Shining River, through the Dark Veils to her paradise. Please…" Suddenly the feeble voice lifted. "I cannot pull out my sword. I have not the strength. Will you do it?"

"So the goddess will see?" Brak said.

The soldier's head bobbed a little. In the gloom Brak could smell weltering blood, and it was warm on his fingers as he loosed the small sword from the man's scabbard, then curled the fingers of the charioteer's cooling hand around it.

Brak felt helpless, baffled. "What more can I do? I cannot leave you here to die without help."

"No help is possible," the soldier replied weakly. "But that is no matter, because now—the Horned Lady will know. Would that I could repay you. The tones in which you speak—they're strange to me. Are you an outlander?"

"Aye. My name is Brak."

"There is the look of the barbarian about you, though your face is in shadow."

"I am on a long journey from the high steppes."

"May the Horned Lady bless your passage." The charioteer was trembling now.

Aching from his fight with the rock creature, Brak rose. He shook his head in pity and weariness.

The brightly-armored man was dying, and there was nothing he could do.

The big barbarian stood a moment, staring down. In that instant, one of the last feeble rays of the sundown light falling across the blasted rocks illuminated the stark shape of his face.

Brak heard a scrabbling, a moaning at his feet.

"What is wrong?" he said, fearful. "Is a black spell on you?"

"Do not cross the Shining River," the dying man rasped. "Barbarian, do not cross! I see your face for the first time. Turn north again. Turn away."

Was this some brink of the grave madness? Brak's barbaric brows crooked together.

"I cannot understand your meaning. I must ride south."

"Phrixos the Shining River lies south!" the charioteer panted. "I warn you, turn away!"

"Tell me why I must."

"There is a sign on your face. *A sign on your face, of...*"

With a long, rough *aaaaggggh* of breath, the charioteer stiffened. His heels drummed once, no more.

Brak shook his head and went to find his pony. He ached. He did not understand the man's wild words. Besides, how could he turn away? He was bound to seek his fortune in the warm climes of Khurdisan far southward.

Weeks ago, Brak had left the ruined hell city of Chambalor with the girl Dareet as his responsibility. Their journey out of the waste took many days. Finally they reached a city lying south of the huge desert but north of this land. In that city Brak bade Dareet farewell, turning her over to the care of a distant cousin, a successful merchant of hides and skins.

Brak then asked directions of an old seer in the city's public market. The crabbed old man drew a sand map with the point of his crook. He sketched a long, scrawling line that was Phrixos, a river he said Brak must eventually cross if his journey's end lay south in golden Khurdisan. War and rumors of war lay in that direction also, and fearsome peoples. The ancient one wheezed that they might well take Brak's life by means of sword or sorcery if he were not quick of wit and swift of blade.

A river, then. He must cross. Phrixos the Shining was its name. Wearily Brak climbed onto his pony's back. Surely what the charioteer had said was only the delirium of death.

He clucked to the pony. They went jogging up the watercourse. Brak was eager to be away from the dead rock monster and the dead charioteer who had seen his face in scarlet light and cried warning.

A sign on his face? What sign?

No matter. Brak knew he must cross Phrixos. There would be no threat.

Yet as he rode through the ominous black land in the new starlight, the smoke floating in the southern sky grew thicker. So did his sense of danger.

The next night Brak slept on a haunted battlefield. All during that day, the day following his encounter with the charioteer, he had ridden across the burned plain here the armies of the kingdom of Phrixos had beaten back those of the hairy men of Gat.

By dawn Brak had reached the near border of this field of carnage; a border marked by a pile of corpses of squat, bandy-legged men in leathern armor. Their flesh was thickly haired, their jawbones thrusting and bestial. Even glazed in death, their eyes were small and mean.

He chanced upon the pile of corpses as his pony rounded a low outcrop. He was passing fewer and fewer of these cairns as he rode. He had come down out of the obsidian wilderness, and now the land leveled and sloped away, as though toward a river delta.

The size of the plain of war was difficult to determine. Many baggage vans and silken pavilions had evidently been torched in the fighting. These still-smoldering ruins filled the sky with the smoke Brak had glimpsed far off. As Brak rode past the corpses, the smoke grew so acrid that vision was difficult beyond a few paces. The pony shied often.

At highest noon, the sun was but a pale silver-white disk through the murk overhead. Everywhere lay bodies, whole or dismembered, stinking of blood that mingled with the richer, redder stuff bled out of horses slaughtered by the hundreds. Brak saw grisly remains of units of foot soldiers, of mounted horse, the wreckage of war engines, and of all the paraphernalia of a gigantic combat.

The ground beneath the pony's hooves was loamy. This silt partially covered many of the bodies. But it was evident that the army of Gat had suffered decisive defeat, for the numbers of its dead far outweighed those in metal armor bearing the device of The Horned Lady.

Still, the kingdom of Phrixos had not escaped lightly, either.

Riding in the smoke all the day long, Brak occasionally heard a moan of pain from some survivor. Twice he reined in. Twice he attempted to locate the source of the cry. Each time, tricks of illusive gray light, of shifting smoke, of silk banners tattered but flapping, bedeviled him. Each time he became hopelessly lost, and failed to locate the wounded man.

On three other occasions, Brak passed ghostly parties of men silently crossing the battleground. The men carried tapers that winked eerily in the blowing smoke. They hallooed to one another. Burial parties from

Phrixos? So Brak assumed. He avoided these groups by remaining immobile on his pony until they had passed out of earshot. Then he picked his way ahead.

The more he rode, the more the big barbarian disliked the route. He felt, somehow, like a scavenger, like one of the monstrous ivory-beaked birds that now and then wheeled down out of the smoke to caw and pluck away a dead eye or bit of flesh. But despite his loathing for this endless array of the dead, he recognized an essential fact of his situation.

In his travels he had known both thick and fat purses. At the moment the little pouch tied by a thong to the lion's-hide garment at his waist was empty of dinshas. Brak cared nothing for coin, but on occasion found it a necessity.

Thus he kept a sharp eye out. He planned to set aside his scruples momentarily when the occasion arose. He would set aside the somewhat unclean feeling the very notion caused in him, so that he might search for a booty, some valuable trinket or item of war he might later barter for food or shelter.

He found the pickings slim as he rode. The sun slipped down. He saw a jeweled sword a-gleaming beyond a burned baggage van. But when he dismounted and approached, he discovered the weapon was sticking up from the backbone of a soldier of Phrixos.

Brak knew that, in worldly terms, he might be counted a fool. Yet he did not have the stomach to violate the dead so thoroughly. He rode on, empty-handed.

The plain continued to slope downward beneath Brak's pony. The sky darkened. A breeze sprang up, stirring the smoke from a thousand fires. The stench of burning had become noxious in Brak's nostrils. He hoped the wind would clear the air.

He found the going more difficult as darkness came on. Soon he decided that he must camp the night. Phrixos the Shining River was farther away than he had anticipated.

At last he settled upon a low hillside where he'd chanced on the remains of a great silken pavilion. Its poles had collapsed. Its fine hangings were already half covered by blowing silt. He climbed down from his pony. The light was failing, which was a blessing of sorts, for it obscured the landscape of corpses.

Brak used several of the snapped halves of pavilion poles to erect a small shelter consisting of scraps of vermilion and gold silk. As he worked, he noticed marks in the earth that indicated that burial searchers had already passed this way. Fresh animal tracks, plus the imprints of crude digging tools, showed that some person of importance had died at this site. Much attention had been given to turning the earth in the vicinity.

Brak's broadsword worked handily to hack some cedar-wood spokes from a split van wheel. Brak piled the spokes up in a cupped place in the earth, struck fire and blew until he had a small blaze going. Hunched over this, a barbaric, melancholy figure, he munched on a bit of tough meat from his pouch.

Then, laying one hand upon his broadsword haft and pulling another ripped swath of vermilion silk over his upper body, he rolled over on his side and tried to sleep.

Whether he dreamed or woke, he did not at first know.

Gigantic armies clashed on a misty plain. Screams arose. He heard moans of torment, and the funeral chanting of tens of thousands of massed voices. Suddenly he sat up.

The darkness had thickened around him. Points of fire danced in his eyes. These he recognized as the last, smoldering coals of the blaze he had built. The vermilion silk fell away from his shoulders as he scrambled lithely to his feet, listening.

Somewhere on the other side of the silken barrier he had erected, something stirred, rustling across the earth. Brak's palm chilled on the broadsword haft.

The sky had cleared while he slept. A few crystal stars were visible, and in the heavens only occasional tatters of smoke drifted now. Smudged grayish light over eastward indicated dawn was quite near.

The wind had a chilly nip in this cold, ghostly hour. Brak's temporary shelter flapped and snapped in an occasional gust. The wind had blown hard enough, Brak saw, to wipe out the traces of the searchers, and reshaped the loamy soil into new mounds and depressions.

Quite suddenly, he heard a voice calling from beyond the sheltering silks.

"Close, so very close—beloved? I have come a long way on the search. I sense the spirit close enough to touch."

A woman's voice!

No mistaking the rich, sorrow-haunted tone, full of eerie echoes, but somehow not quite real. Brak's savage face wrenched into a scowl of puzzlement. His empty belly turned colder.

Something about the voice was unnatural.

Half-crouched, he moved to his left with deliberate slowness. This path would bring him out from behind the shelter. In a moment he would be able to see what lurked on the other side.

The voice rose up, now faint, now compellingly louder. The big barbarian had the wild notion that, somehow, he was hearing weeping that had been articulated into words: "Across this plain of woe they have hunted. And come back to say the butchers of Gat worked too well. That nothing remains to be borne beside me through the Dark Veils. It costs me pain to come searching across the night, beloved, but I bear it, for I must find you. Else the river will be dark and paradise empty. *I know they are wrong, I know you can be found. Close now I feel a spirit, its warmth.*"

So oddly clear was that voice, that Brak almost expected to look beyond the shelter and find a woman standing there. To see that area fully, he would have to move another pace to the left. Carefully he shifted his weight. The long, savage braid bobbed gently against his naked backbone.

His left foot struck something sharp. Glancing down, Brak saw a dull-gilt gleam in the uncertain light. The wind sighed. Without thinking, he reached down toward the gleam. His fingers closed around the rolled metal edge of something very heavy.

He tugged. From beneath an accumulation of wind-blown silt, a great shield came free.

Just as Brak pulled up the shield, the wind gave a gust. One of the hastily-rigged support posts toppled over. One by one the sheltering silks streamed away like enchanted flags.

Brak stood rooted with his forearm slipped through the leathern loops on the inner side of the shield as the last silk blew away and he saw her.

Tiny beating pains began in his temples. He was sure he was mad.

The woman searching the dark plain was slim, regal, lovely, and of a relatively young age. Her locks were dark and down to her waist. But they floated out behind her with a weird undersea motion.

Already the stars had paled. Dawn was very close. There was enough light for Brak to see that the woman's arms, widespread and supplicating, were soft and white. Her gown was of an even purer white, except at her breast. Brak's mind chilled, an evil black clot of blood appeared on her breast, long dried now, but so large, it must have been the mortal wound.

Brak sensed somehow that the young woman was royal. She bore herself so. But where her gown should have revealed the tips of slippers, there was only blackish mist.

Through her face, her body, through the dark eyes turning toward him suddenly, Brak saw *the sky and starlight.*

He brought the shield up instinctively. Out of the wind came a sudden sighing: "They did not search well enough. I have found you. Your face is strange, not quite the same. And yet you have the great shield."

With a stir of strange mists, the ghostly girl seemed to float closer to Brak. "Quickly, beloved! Stretch out your hand. Touch mine. *Then we will leave together.*"

Closer the ghost-girl floated, sad and smiling. *Closer.*

The big barbarian was helpless. How could he strike at a wraith? Yet he sensed that once those transparent fingers touched his body he would be as she was.... Dead.

"Beloved? *Beloved, come touch me.* No longer will the bier beside mine be empty."

The outstretched fingers were near Brak's shoulder, nearly touching.

A line of corpses nearby suddenly flushed rosy. Brak swallowed violently. Eyes squeezed shut for an instant, he shook his head. There was a wild swirling of cold wind all about. A sad, forlorn wail.

Brak opened his eyes again. He was alone on the little hilltop, save for the tumbled grotesqueries of the piled-up dead lying pink in the gleam of the sun on the eastern horizon.

Who was she? Why had she wanted him? Because of the shield? The big barbarian turned it slowly in his hands.

Not brass at all, he saw with a gasp. He fingered the rich bossing. Gold! Purest beaten gold, worked with strange

devices. At the center, a shining bas-relief of The Horned Lady stood out. Brak had seen other weapons lying discarded on the battlefield. He had seen nothing so fine as this anywhere.

To whom had it belonged? A prince? A king? He was tempted to throw it away. Then he remembered his empty pouch.

Perhaps the shield was a sacred article. Perhaps it could be redeemed in one of the cities of Phrixos for a night's lodgings and a parcel of food. Gradually the deepening daylight, the thinning smoke, helped dispel his fright at having encountered the fleshless, dead-yet-living beauty.

Had he dreamed it all? There was not a mark upon the silted earth where a mark should have been had her body been solid.

Again Brak weighed the situation. His fortune seemed to have taken another, ominous turn. Still the conclusion he reached was inescapable. He had no choice but to press on and cross the River Phrixos, for in that direction lay the goal of his journey.

He kicked out the last embers of his dead fire and climbed up onto his pony's back. He looped the carrying thong of the great shield over his left shoulder so that the shield hung slanted across his mighty back. Riding, he soon passed into a grove, away from the field of battle.

Even though it was full morning, a kind of dappled twilight enfolded him in the grove. A bird with red eyes swooped past, cawing cruelly. Brak gnawed his lip. He tried to recall what the girl's haunted voice had called to him. Something about his face being strange, not quite the same.

The same as what? With a shudder, he remembered the charioteer's talk of a sign.

Prudence cautioned him to cast the mighty curved shield aside. He was hungry, and was anxious to be on his way southward. So he rode ahead, soon emerging from the grove.

He wended his way down rutted paths past rude huts squatting among fertile croplands. Far away to his right, the spires of a city shone. He was more interested in what lay before him, however.

In the distance, just discernible, sparkled the silver thread of a river in the sunlight.

Brak clucked to his pony and jogged ahead. The distances played tricks. He had ridden for almost all of the day by the time he finally caught sight of the shoreline.

The river was plain now. A great shining span of lead-colored water, it ran from right to left, horizon to horizon, flanked on either bank by pleasant pastoral fields. The land had a more decided slant here, tilting down to the nearer shore.

And upon this shore some distance directly ahead, Brak saw a sleepy, sprawling inn, and a sagging pier. At the pier a ferryman's barge was tied up, bobbing empty on the waters of the Shining River in the dusk.

That barge would be his means of escaping from this strange, bewitched kingdom.

Great gold warshield still looped across his brawny back, the big barbarian made haste toward the inn and pier on the shore side of Phrixos. He had gone only a short way when he reined in abruptly.

Midway between him and his destination, the rutted track that bore the marks of cottager's wheels intersected a broader highway. This highway was contracted of massive interlocked squares of bluish stone. It wound away along the riverbank on Brak's right hand. Undoubtedly it led to the city whose pinnacles alternately glimmered and hid behind fast-blowing clouds in the distance.

A party of half-a-dozen armed horsemen had appeared along this paved highway, coming from Brak's left in the lowering twilight.

Cautiously Brak kneed the pony forward. He and the horsemen would reach the junction at approximately the same time. Brak's stomach tensed.

The men were clearly soldiers. Oddly garbed soldiers, though; behind each man fluttered a black and yellow barred cape, reminding Brak of tiger hides he had seen displayed in market places along the route of his journey.

These sinister tiger cloaks whipped out in the wind as the riders flashed along. Their swords clanked. They were an ominous pack in the waning light, mean-faced men, all mounted on splendid glistening black horses with fierce rolling white eyes. The stark sameness of their black mounts and clothing, relieved only by the yellow striped cloaks, told Brak that the men must be retainers of some lord's great house in the neighborhood.

Though Brak did not shrink from meeting the men, he recognized that he was an outlander, and little would be gained by drawing attention to himself. So he hung back slightly, holding the pony's reins tight in. He intended to let the riders clatter past the intersection unimpeded.

The horsemen came ahead at full gallop. The hooves of their wild black horses struck hissing green and silver sparks from the huge paving stones.

Hunched over on his pony Brak dawdled along, keeping one eye upon the ferry station down by the riverbank.

That was his destination. To cross the River Phrixos was his main purpose. Better to avoid a confrontation.

Still, something in him seemed to stir and rebel at the sight of the shouting pack of bravos storming along the highway. Brak was irritated by this unfounded anger. Although he was a barbarian, his travels and adventures had taught him the virtue of prudence in certain situations.

So he attempted to blend into the shadows of evening as the retainers thundered into the cross-roads. It was the big barbarian's ill luck that one of the riders chanced to look in his direction.

Immediately the man sawed on his reins. His black mount skidded and stamped to a stop. More sparks showered and spurted from his iron-shod hoofs. The man raised a black gauntlet to point.

The others reined in, tiger cloaks flapping. One of the men was taller than the others. He had a thin, pinched white face between the jawflaps of his leathern helmet. He cupped a glove to call: "Outlander! Stranger! Ride a piece closer. We'd have a word with you."

Brak hesitated. His hand dropped toward the haft of his broadsword. He was acutely conscious of the weight of the great gold shield across his back. He tensed his knees against the pony's flanks, trying to decide what to do. Among the retainers there was a loud clack of talk and comment, and much craning in the saddle to see, for the light was rapidly going out of the cloud-blown sky.

"Doubtless he's just some clod vagabond, captain," Brak heard one of the retainers say loudly. "And the evening shadows can play tricks."

"Nay, I had a fair shot at his face," replied the man who had first sighted Brak. Quickly he snaked out a narrow, wickedly bright sword. "He's not a perfect match. Still, 'tis close enough that…" The man realized Brak had not gigged his pony forward. "You! Did you hear? Ride over to us this moment."

Another retainer nudged his captain. "What's that upon his back?"

Carefully Brak drew out his broadsword. He waited, sitting unmoving on his pony in the middle of the rutted road.

"On his back?"

The captain craned up in the saddle. Then he sank quickly down again and gave a shudder. Onto his face flashed a look of pure terror. A moment later, Brak realized the man must have identified the configuration on the shield, for Brak's pony had shied a little, and half-turned in the track. The elaborate gold bossing would be dimly visible from the highway.

"The Horned Lady protect us!" came the captain's shaky voice. "He must be some scavenger of the dead. He's carrying the warshield of Nicor."

Among the black-booted riders, this statement set off a pandemonium of whispers and hasty signs against evil eye. One of the men, however, was a bit bolder than the others.

"If that's so, I can't see the cursed thing clearly, then we ought to chop off his blasphemous hands and take it back." With an iron whisper, the man's sword came free.

"Hold!"

Even after the command, the retainer kept urging his ebony-colored horse forward toward the highway's edge. Quickly the captain slashed his own blade down on the man's forearm, making the bravo howl.

"I said hold!" cried the captain, reaching out to grasp the other man's rein. He jerked so violently that the retainer was nearly tumbled from the saddle. "I will not put my hands upon that shield and neither will you." Then the captain bawled to Brak, "Outlander! Put up your sword. Ride over here. No harm will come to you."

It was natural for Brak to suspect treachery behind the promise. He kept the broadsword ready, laid across his powerful thighs as he urged the pony on. If he did not bluff them out, he risked a fight, a chase, or worse. The most prudent course seemed also the most direct.

As he jogged to the crossroad, Brak noticed that the looks of awe and apprehension directed at the gigantic shield on his back were genuine. The riders actually hung back, with a kind of strained respect. Swords had been sheathed.

The hooves of Brak's pony clacked loud and sharp on the blue paving of the highway as he drew up before the riders. They studied him carefully. They took in his huge frame, the savage yellow braid hanging down his mighty back, the lion's hide at his waist.

"I was right indeed to call you outlander," the captain said. "You come a far distance."

Brak was still tense, but less so than he had been a moment before. "Aye. And my only intent is to pass on without trouble."

"Where are you bound?"

"Khurdisan in the far south."

There were murmurs. "That's a long way to go," said the captain. He paused. Then, carefully: "Where did you come by that shield?"

"Upon the battlefield I rode across," Brak replied. "I discovered it fairly, and I claim it as spoil. If it belongs to someone important in your land, I'm willing to barter it for food and a few coins."

The captain laughed uneasily. "For a barbarian, you have a sharp trading sense, anyway."

"To whom does the shield belong?" Brak asked. "Someone slaughtered in the battle?"

The corners of the captain's mouth tightened. "It's of no matter. On closer inspection, I see 'tis not the shield we thought it was at all."

Brak knew the man lied. The answer was too flat and swift. Nervous, gemlike black eyes flicking across Brak's face. The captain gave a wave of his ebony gauntlet, "Aye, we were mistaken."

His sharp glance wiped away the sudden looks of surprise on the faces of his men. The captain turned his horse's head aside, deferentially, but with a certain subtle menace that Brak did not miss.

"You may pass on, outlander. We beg your pardon for troubling you. As one of my men observed, 'tis this twilight that plays tricks. May the gods put strong winds at your back to carry you to your destination."

And with a thin, insincere smile! playing on his lips, the captain nudged his horse further out of the way. Brak had a clear passage across the highway.

The big barbarian did not hesitate. He clucked to the pony and clattered off.

Once back on the rutted track, Brak sent the pony ahead full speed, following the downward slope. Several persons were stirring in the inn yard by the pier. A lantern shutter opened suddenly, spreading a fan of yellow light across the dirt of the yard. Brak rode a distance more, then slowed and turned around.

Up on the highway, the retainers were still watching him, sinister black figures against the reddening horizon line. Brak knew that the captain's last words to him had been deceptive. And he somehow knew that he carried upon his back a warshield belonging to an important personage. The sooner he got rid of it, and traveled across the River Phrixos, the safer he would be.

The wind stirred his long braid eerily as he watched the silhouetted riders on the highway. Suddenly there was a barked command. The company of men spurred away into the distance, sparks and tiger-blazed cloaks flying behind them.

Brak watched until they were out of sight. Then he turned and started toward the inn and pier. Suddenly he shouted in dismay and kicked the pony savagely ahead.

"Ferryman! Hold your barge to shore! Ho! Listen to me...." It was too late.

In the interval during which Brak had watched the road, several persons emerging from the inn had climbed aboard the rickety barge, and the ferryman was already poling them out across the River Phrixos, in the! general direction of a small cluster of lights that marked a village on the opposite bank.

Brak's pony thundered into the inn yard. Lantern in hand, a greasy fat man with an immense reddish beard and a soiled leather apron was just preparing to return indoors. Brak leaped down from the pony's back.

"Landlord, call the barge back. I wish to cross."

The bearded man lifted the swaying light. "It cannot be done, stranger. There are no more crossings once the light fails. At dawn, he will be back."

Beams from the lantern spilled across Brak's face. Gilt highlights glittered and flashed from the rolled edge of the shield slung across Brak's back. The landlord turned the color of cooked grain in a meal pot.

"Where did you get...?" he began. Then, without warning, he made a cabalistic sign. "We have no room here. We're full to the rafters. You'll have to ride on." He turned away toward the entrance to his dilapidated and obviously empty place of business.

By now Brak's fury and puzzlement were out of bounds. He leaped forward. He seized the landlord's shoulder and spun him around, thrusting the shuddering man bodily against the wall.

"Landlord, I'm sick of the mooning and eye rolling and gasps and shudders I find every time I encounter a human being in this cursed country. I want food, and a sack of wine, and a place to stretch out for the night. I want passage across this river. In return, you can have this tinnish toy that seems to arouse so much interest."

Brak unlooped the shield and would have thrust it at the landlord, had not the latter thrown up his hands and sidled crabwise along the wall, as if he feared to touch the gold-bossed thing.

"No, no keep it! I could not. That is, I don't want it. Sleep in the stables if you want. I'll see that you get some food. Just don't pollute my—don't enter my house, I beg you." The landlord's face seemed to dissolve into lardy softness as he whined away, "We have had enough woe in Phrixos, we need no more."

His hand indicated a patch of clack mourning-cloth pegged to the inn door. He kept glancing back and forth from the great gold war shield to Brak's face. In the glow of the lantern, the man's skin glistened with sweat that ran down in his great red beard. The poor oaf was virtually blubbering!

Brak tried to conceal his contempt: "Landlord?"

"'What?"

"Am I scarred?"

"I don't understand."

"Am I some monstrosity? What is upon my face that so affrights everyone? And who is this Nicor I heard about?"

"Nicor! Blasphemy, blasphemy! Oh, gods, I will be punished."

"Nicor owned this shield. Who was he?"

The landlord tried to pull away again, snuffling.

Brak whipped out his broadsword. "You blubbering fat calf! I'll split you from neck to hip if you don't stop wailing and tell me."

The landlord gave another fierce pull, darted to the side and managed to get inside the building and slam the door. A latch rattled.

Brak heard the river's soft lapping at the edge of the rotting pier behind him. A frenzied, frightened eye looked out of a peephole in the door, to see if Brak had disappeared. Then a shadow blurred across the dimly-lit window. The landlord made wild motions, directing Brak away from the building.

The big barbarian uttered a soft but heartfelt curse. He shouldered the golden shield and tramped off, broadsword in hand, to find the stable and some fodder for his pony.

A lanthorn provided some light within the smelly stable building. Brak fed and bedded his mount. While he was doing so, the landlord evidently crept out of the inn and back inside again, for Brak eventually noticed some objects lying in the stable doorway: an earthenware vessel, and a platter with a joint of meat and a butt of grayish bread on it.

Ravenous, Brak devoured the bread, meat, and thin, sour wine. He wiped his mouth with his forearm. He was beginning to shake off his uneasiness. Being feared—for whatever the reason—had some advantages. No doubt the landlord had been willing to feed him to keep him out of the inn proper.

Settling down in a fragrant pile of hay with his broadsword beside his leg, Brak blew out the lanthorn. He reflected idly upon these latest peculiar circumstances. But weariness soon swept over him. Perhaps he was eager for the advent of dawn and the return of the ferryman; he wanted to escape from this fear-crazed kingdom. Sleep would hasten time.

He yawned and closed his eyes.

And during the night, while Brak slept, they trapped him.

He awoke to a clink of armored trappings, a stamp of hooves, gleams and reflections of lantern light. There was a sudden halloo, and the rush of a great hemped spider-webbing dropping down over his huge body.

With a cry he was up. He slashed and chopped the broadsword at the immense, heavy net that had been cast over him by shadowy figures he glimpsed clinging up high on the stable's rafters.

"Get that sword away from him!" a man's harsh voice commanded. "But make no wounds!"

Brak slashed, clubbed, fought. He was not fully awake. His eyes were bleary. Men ran round and round him, wrapping him tighter and tighter in the strands of the great net. He cut one cable, then another, then a third. He tried to lunge out through the opening. A spear came whipping at his head.

The impact was brutal. He went to his knees. More folds of the net closed around him.

Suddenly a boot stamped down on his outstretched hand. His broadsword was wrenched away. He was jerked over on his back and lifted, dizzyingly, as a rope-wheel creaked. The net was cranked and lifted up and away from the stable floor.

Stifled, with a huge strand of the net cable binding mercilessly tight across his face, Brak hung swaying in the net, directly in front of two people who had ridden into the stable and now sat their horses as men on foot scurried around them, weapons bared and bright in the glow of fluttering torches.

A hoarse, wordless cry of rage tore from Brak's throat, because the net cable was so tight across his face. He saw the livery of two dozen men who filled the stable and clung goblinlike to the rafters. They were clad in black from helmet to boots, and wore flamboyant tiger-hide cloaks.

The man who led them was one of the two persons on horseback. He was tall, slender, and unhealthy looking. He had a whiplike strength that came across in the way he leaned forward to poke the point of his thin, wicked sword through the netting and against Brak's ribs.

The swordsman was clad like his servants. But a single ornament set him apart; a clasp made from a huge tiger's claw. It held his cape at his right shoulder. The man twisted his hand slightly, touching the blade's sharp point to Brak's flesh. The metal was stained a dark rusty color half the length of its flat side.

"We do not know your name, barbarian. I am called Hel, Lord of the Tigers. It is on behalf of her highness that I am acting."

The man indicated the second rider, a woman seated on a white charger beside him. Though wearing an emerald cloak, veil, and partial facecloth, the woman could still be seen to bear a startling resemblance to the ghostly girl Brak had encountered on the battlefield. She was dark, lustrous eyed, and heartbreakingly lovely.

Still, she seemed strangely uncertain seated on her splendid mount there beside the cruel, commanding figure of the lord called Hel, who spoke again.

"I suppose I owe you some explanation, lout." The Lord spoke conversationally, as if he talked every day to a huge savage trussed and hanging before him in a net. "'Tis simple enough. Queen Rhea here rules Phrixos of the Shining River now that her older sister, Queen Joenna, has perished on the battlefield. She died when our armies routed the men of Gat. The husband of Queen Joenna, Prince Nicor, was likewise killed in the conflict. Unfortunately his body was not recovered. In order that the ceremonies and augurs may be fulfilled, so that Queen Rhea's reign may be established, the bodies of both Joenna and Nicor must be sent down the river through the Dark Veils to paradise. Otherwise the priests will take new omens and search another royal house for a ruler. And that, of course, is why my men, whom you met on the highroad, came riding to tell us of the twist of circumstance that had brought you here, for reasons I can't guess and frankly don't care about. My men did say that you are traveling to Khurdisan. Rather, you were."

Lord Hel chuckled. It had a cold, malicious sound. Queen Rhea leaned over to him.

"Lord, if we must engage in this kind of wicked sport, at least let it be done quickly. He is an innocent man. He knows nothing of our customs."

Irritated, Lord Hel twisted in his saddle. The nails of the tiger-claw clasp at his shoulder glinted with a dead ivory paleness.

"Forgive me if I call those words unseemly, my queen. I trust you realize the size of the stakes involved. Your rule hangs upon the completion of the ritual. It hangs upon your sister's body, and the body of her husband Nicor, entering paradise together on the holy barge. We already have Joenna's corpse embalmed. Now we have our Nicor as well."

"I don't care for your tone, Lord. You presume too much."

"My lady, I only..."

"You also display a certain greedy eagerness to trick the people into believing that we have recovered Prince Nicor's body."

"My lady, it is to your advantage!" Hel said, irritated.

"And to yours, now that the priests have betrothed us?"

The Lord of the Tigers shrugged eloquently. "As you will, my queen. I have no regrets about using this stranger to fulfill the desired end. By chance he has found Nicor's sacred warshield when our searchers could not. And by an even greater stroke of luck, he is well suited for the purpose. The palace cosmeticians will have little to do on him."

"And you have no scruples as well as no regrets, Lord?"

"None, my lady. Your rule depends upon our success. Besides, whoever the outlander is, he should be pleased. Somewhere, in whatever pigsty land spawned him, his gods smiled. 'Tis not every hulk who can play the part of a royal consort's corpse. Eh, barbarian?"

And, with a jingle of black trappings, Lord Hel rode closer to where Brak hung helpless in the net.

From his tunic Hel removed something round and golden. He held it up close to where Brak's fevered eye looked out through the net's crisscross. Tight trussed, Brak remembered many things then.

The words of the charioteer. The ghostly voice of the spectral queen searching, searching the battlefield for her husband, her coruler.

Against a background of the pale, upturned faces of Hel's retainers, Brak saw the thing the Lord held. It was a round coin inscribed along its border with unfamiliar characters. The coin twinkled in the torchlight.

On the side at which Brak looked, a woman's face was struck. It was a face much like that of Queen Rhea. It was the face of the dead queen whom Brak had met on the haunted field.

Another twinkle, and Hel reversed the coin. His bright, dark eyes were full of foul amusement.

"Look well, barbarian. You should be honored."

On the coin's opposite side, another head had been raised, this time that of a man. Undoubtedly he was Nicor, the dead Joenna's consort.

Prisoned within the net, Brak writhed in fright and horror.

The face of the man on the coin was almost identically Brak's own.

Strange mists of unconsciousness began to shred and part. And Brak heard a cacophony of weird, marrow-chilling sounds.

The first was the high, piercing ring within his own ears. It brought absolute agony.

He lay stiff. His eyes were closed on a darkness full of subtly shifting flickers of light. Somehow, he felt that a great deal of time had passed, perhaps as much as several days and nights, since he had hung trussed in the net. He remembered...

Almost magically, Hel, Lord of the Tigers, had made the twinkling coin disappear into his black doublet.

Then, with a clap of gauntlets, Hel summoned a crabbed, white-locked, sandaled old man to his side. The elderly shaman had been lurking back in the gloomy depths of the stable, awaiting the signal. His voluminous russet sackcloth robe rustled as he began to move his hands and mutter incomprehensible incantations just below the net.

Suddenly, with one of his long-nailed hands, the shaman plucked something from the folds of his begrimed garment. His lips writhed as he mumbled. He had the wild, rolling-eyed look of the alchemical priest, the holy madman.

The big barbarian remembered what the aged one had lifted to rake along his exposed flank as he hung in the net. It was a rusty, fishhook-shaped needle, multi-barbed and glistening with a thick, iridescent yellow gum. At the first prick, the gummy potion immediately produced the awful ringing in Brak's ears. He was overcome with such leaden stiffness, that he was unable to do so much as shift a limb after a bit.

As Brak passed from consciousness, the last thing he saw was a torchlit cameo of two faces: one was Hel's, smugly satisfied; the other was Queen Rhea's. She was in the background, and still looked uncertain, as if she disliked this charlatan's scheme to keep power.

So now, as Brak again grew aware of the awl-sharp ringing inside his head, he felt a red fury, mingled with a sense of deep dread. Very likely he was doomed.

He attempted to shift his arms. He could not. He could not move them so much as a fraction. They seemed to lie like wood logs at his sides. A feeling of terror and frustration welled inside of him.

In his ears, many wild sounds beat. He knew he was still in the grip of the drug, whatever it was. His heart thudded faster in panic.

Calm, calm! he cried at himself silently. There was a sensation of undulating motion. Instantly he knew he was aboard some gently-moving vessel upon water. *Calm now,* he thought. *You've strength enough to open your eyes, if only you want to. Do that much, to learn where you are. Then find a sword. A sword to take you out of this...this* dead place.

Brak could feel that he had no broadsword strapped at his hip, for the lingering, ear-piercing effects of the drug left him dully aware of the state of his brawny body, even though he had no control over it. He was lying horizontally. Odd-feeling silks and linens were wrapped around his torso, his lower body. His arms felt heavy with metal ornaments.

And in his nostrils rose a stench like the stench he had smelled once in a great city through which he'd passed on the day a royal heir died.

The stench came from the sweetish unguents of embalmers.

Overcome suddenly by total terror, Brak flashed his eyes open. He stared from his stretched-out position into a shimmering, blazing, blowing wall of fire.

Orange tatters blazed and burned. Seconds passed. Brak's mind focused with less alarm on the flaming wall. Its individual components separated, grew more distinct.

He was gazing obliquely down a row of torches, closely spaced. Each torch was inserted in a socket at the top of a high ivory pole twice as tall as a man.

Then the sounds... The sounds bedeviled him. But these, too, gradually sorted themselves. First there was the wet, restless purling of a watercraft moving down the river. He heard the restless bubble of a prow slowly, lazily breaking the way in a current that bore the vessel along. And he heard a clash of bells, a mutter and thudding of drums. The music mingled with a high, thin wail as of a eunuch priest chanting.

All this was in the distance, overlaid with an occasional roar of laughter, a babble of voices with the incongruous sound of revelry.

Finally, Brak heard a far-off massed song, as of ten times ten thousand voices raised in some hymn. All around him floated the cloying scent of blooms, of incense curling green from censers, of the embalmer's unguents upon his body.

He found that he was growing less and less paralyzed with each passing second; was the drug failing?

With an aching exertion, he found he could roll onto his left shoulder. He looked, and gasped and gnawed hard on his own lips to sting himself back to sanity.

The scene did not vanish.

Brak lay upon a high, golden catafalque. It rested in turn upon the stem castle of a great, wide barge. The ivory-poled torches were planted in two rows down the rails. Beyond the row on his left, Brak saw the dark water of the River Phrixos reflecting highlights of yellow and vermilion from the barge's torches, lanterns, and lamps.

Looking harder, Brak saw that the shape of the land had changed. This suggested that the barge had been in passage! for some time.

Despite the darkness, Brak could make out some detail Instead of low delta shores, steep bluffs reared. Their summits were defined by thousands upon thousands of pinpricks of fire.

Torches…

Suddenly, every detail flooded back. The barbarian realized who he was, or was not. From the distant shore', lying as he was, bathed in torchlight, he would look like the man whose body was supposed to be journeying down the river to paradise beyond the Dark Veils.

He was Prince Nicor, aboard the death barge. From the bluffs, citizens of Phrixos watched the vessel's passage, and countless voices chanted a funeral hymn.

Escape! That was what counted now. Escape from the tangles of this cursed plot, this evil deception. Brak found that he could lift his left leg. Gripping the edge of the catafalque, he tried to swing his lower body down from it. As he turned his head, his gaze fell upon his own hand. Aghast, he held it up before his eyes.

The flesh was bone white. He sniffed. Dimly, he remembered Hel mentioning palace cosmeticians. For a moment he wanted to cackle with savage, disbelieving laughter. He was a dead man, tricked out in a dead man's robes, his skin whitened to a corpselike paleness.

Abruptly Brak jerked his hand down again. He lay still as granite, staring straight up at a great peacock-hued canopy that hung above the catafalque. The multicolored hangings of this silken pavilion were drawn back to allow the shore watchers to glimpse the dead bodies bound for paradise. He should not have raised his hand to his face. Someone might have seen from shore.

No outcry disturbed the singing. Brak relaxed a little, but remained stiff on his back. It would not be wise just yet to treat the watchers to the sight of the dead rising.

The dead... Another cold shiver crawled up his back. He was but a consort. He was some swaggering prince named Nicor, married to...

Brak wrenched his head far enough to the right so that he could see for the first time what lay in that direction. There, upon a similar catafalque, rested the robed body of Queen Joenna.

Her eyelids were a pale bluish color, closed in death. Her hands were folded upon her breast. Her lips had been tinted coral. A simple pearl chaplet adorned her head. Beyond her, more torches were ranked along the starboard rail. On that far bluff, too, thousands sang, and lined the night with fire dots as far as the eye could see.

A foreboding of evil filled Brak then. The queen lay dead. The same queen whose cold, translucent self he had encountered on the battlefield as she searched for het husband's body.

Where was that haunted spirit now?

Close, very close. Brak sensed it. Her soul might be hovering within that pale ivory body that was stretched out unmoving, and yet seemed (had the gods made him mad?) subtly *alive*.

Floating down Phrixos on a timber-hewn island of light, Brak felt more helpless than he ever had in his life. True, most of his lassitude was drained away now. But he had no weapon. The moment he left the catafalque, thousands upon the shores would see, and cry out.

Cautiously he inched his head up just enough, so that he could peer past the tight, binding toes of the calfskin boots that had been jammed onto his feet. He wanted to assess the size of the barge, the number of persons aboard.

The big barbarian judged the barge to be the most immense he had ever seen. He translated the size into an easy, familiar scale of reckoning. It was perhaps as long as a hundred great gray elephant bulls standing trunk to tail, and a fourth as wide. Mammoth. The priestly wail, the music, and the clamor of celebrants, came from a tiny patch of light far ahead at the prow.

There, at least three dozen people were gathered in a smaller, lamplit silk pavilion. Wine cups twinkled.

In between bow and stern pavilions, the deck pit of the barge was nearly pitch dark. Once, perhaps, the vessel had been equipped with rower's benches. Now the barge seemed propelled along by the swiftness of the current of Phrixos; no oars or sails were in evidence. And all that was visible in the old oar pit was a small, square stone altar, fitfully lit by three peculiarly shaped lamps on a trident stand. They cast a smoky purple glow.

Near this altar, Brak thought he saw something. A shadow, a lump of living dark stirred and whipped past the wan circle of radiance cast by the altar lights. Then Brak blinked, uncertain.

A gust of wind stirred distant hangings. Brak glimpsed men wearing tiger stripes, there among the revellers in the bow pavilion. Would they be leaving the barge? Undoubtedly, for beyond the Dark Veils, whatever they were, lay the sacred abode of the dead. But the priests and funeral celebrants would need a means to leave the barge at the crucial point. Where was it?

Resting perfectly flat on the catafalque, Brak listened more sharply to the lap of the waters. He heard two separate sounds. One was the lumbering rush and bubble of the great barge in passage. There was also a heavier slap and splatter, as of a smaller craft, like a good-sized punt, being towed.

Blazing brightness behind him attracted Brak's attention. He craned his head back and saw the immense gold war-shield of Prince Nicor suspended by silken cords immediately above and between the two biers. The hanging shield swayed in the wind. The Horned Lady, holding her sheaf and lightning fork, looked down from the great shield with implacable hammered-metal eyes.

"Barbarian!"

The sibilant whisper, made the hairs at the back of Brak's neck prickle. His long, savage braid was wrapped and hidden in some kind of headcloth, which shifted uncomfortably as he twisted his head to the right, toward the sound.

Was the dead queen's spirit moving?

"Barbarian?" The voice came again, husky, emotion-choked, but somehow familiar. "Do not turn your head too far. I crept up from the altar pit."

So he had seen someone moving down there after all.

"Where are you?" he whispered back.

"Hiding down here, crouched between the biers. It's a strange, humiliating position for—for a queen."

Then Brak knew, from only the voice:

"Queen Rhea?"

"Yes."

"Why are you…?"

"Don't question me!" The reply was sharp. Was the girl sobbing? Against the lap of the waves, it was impossible to tell. "I may change my mind, and decide that the preservation of my kingdom is more important than the life of one nameless outlander. Meantime, I've brought something with which you can strike free, if you dare to try. Now I must return. Even the stolen cowl of one of the serving girls won't cover my absence all that long."

"I do not understand this," Brak said. He stared straight up, unmoving, playing the game now. His heart thudded fast within his mighty chest as he peered through the silken hangings overhead at a starry sky where clouds were closing in fast. "I know little enough about this rogue's game, because they drugged me. But I know enough to realize that unless my body goes the full journey on this death barge, the priests will take it as a bad omen. And the throne won't be yours."

"'Tis Hel the Tiger Lord who wants the throne, and me, so badly."

"And you do not want the throne?"

"Of course I do. You crack-brained lout! Do you want me to change my mind and take back what I brought you?"

"No," Brak replied. "But I must understand the reason."

"The reason is, I am fool enough to place value on a human life, even yours. I warn you, waste many more moments talking, and there will be no time for you to leap overboard. We are near the place on the river where the priests and the celebrants must leave. Already the current's picking up. And can you see the sky? Those are the first clouds of the Veils puffing in overhead."

"What are the Veils?"

"Immense clouds forever sitting up the River Phrixos from one bank to the other."

"What lies beyond them?"

"Paradise," she said softly. "Or perhaps hell. A sound of thunder boils out of them. The great clouds spread over the land for leagues all around. It is a holy place, into which no one dares venture. Approaching the Veils by land, you come upon a great, clammy wall of settled cloud. What lies beyond, I cannot say. The area has been sacred since time forgotten. Perhaps the River Phrixos dips and falls into the bowels of the earth inside the Veils. But the priests say it is paradise.

Big fool! Are you going to gabble questions at me without end? My safety is periled too, you know."

Brak gnawed his lip as he lay in the flickering torchlight. "The mourners on the cliffs will cry out when I move."

"So they will. But if you leap into the river, and are strong enough to swim against the current, strong enough to avoid being dragged to the Veils, perhaps you can escape."

"And what of you? What of the throne?"

Her reply, from where she crouched unseen between the biers, was a strange mixture of venom and sadness: "I would not have come, barbarian, if the throne had mattered more than decency. The world is not exclusively made up of Lord Hels, you know. Perhaps that is what I must prove. Joenna, she was always the hard one, the audacious one—the warrior queen. I am younger. And softer, it might be. Once the court necromancers called me a teary-eyed goose. I wept over a young kidling they gored on a feast-day altar. Don't ask me to explain why I'm idiot enough to risk the Horned Lady's wrath, or risk a throne I'm obliged to fill but, in truth, have no real heart for. I've stayed long enough. I must go, I..."

There was a quick little sobbing sound, followed by a rustling. The lovely dark-haired girl rose abruptly from her hiding place. Her features were partly hidden by the rude cowl of her robe. But Brak could see that her cheeks gleamed with the diamond tracks of tears.

Rhea's warm, faintly trembling hand slipped up, touched his chin for a heartbeat of time.

"Must you make me say it all, barbarian? You are like that animal I wept over long ago. I cannot see a thing die when I have a feeling of love for it."

Quickly, she pressed her lips down against his. Then she dropped from sight Brak heard the soft flurry of her movements as she stole down toward the blackness of the altar. Her voice floated back with a last warning: "Swim hard once you leap off the barge. Phrixos runs fast here. Your strength should be returning. The last time they would have pricked your skin to drug you, I deceived them and wiped the needle clean on my hem. May the Horned Lady forgive me for what I have done!"

Silence.

The altar lights guttered and fumed purple down in the old rowing pit as she passed somewhere in the dark.

At once Brak felt a desperate surging of hope. The barge seemed to be picking up momentum. Overhead, through the intervening silks, he saw clouds beginning to fly thick and swiftly. Or was it the barge doing the flying, into the first tatters of the Dark Veils?

The curtains swirled wildly around the catafalques now, as they swirled around the bow pavilion. The wind increased.

Upon Brak's mouth was the sweet-salt memory of the kiss of the girl Rhea. That kiss was explanation enough for the awful conflict that must have raged within her before she decided to risk everything in order to spare him. He must not waste her courage.

Carefully he dropped his right hand over the catafalque's side, reached down, and closed his fingers around the hard iron shaft of his broadsword.

She had brought it! Smuggled under her cape. The gods thank her!

The piercing ring in his ears, caused by the potion of the needle, had waned. Brak knew he could move from the catafalque now. He took a tighter grip on the sword's haft, gulped air, suddenly levered himself up.

He swung over the left side and dropped with a thud of boots to the decking. The deck itself tilted and swayed sharply in the glare of the ivory-poled torches. The barge seemed to be traveling ever more rapidly. The waters of the River Phrixos had grown choppy. Occasional cold cloudlets went streaming past the rail. It was one of these low-skating clouds that shredded apart an instant after Brak leaped to the deck.

His free hand went up to rip the encumbering gem-crusted headcloth away. He shook his long braid loose with a wild, savage bob of his head. The cloud over the water blew away. There was a sudden, growling change in the massed voices from the shore.

It was now a roar, a shout, an alarm. Brak's lips skinned back in a cruel grin. In the pavilion's light, he had jumped from the catafalque. The watchers had seen the dead spring to life.

"Halloo, halloo the barge! Masters? Masters 'ware!" The sudden cry sent Brak racing to the rail. The voice belonged to a tiger-cloaked functionary dimly glimpsed down by the welter of foam off the port bow. There, tied and plunging at the end of a thick hemp, was a smaller barge. The man who had shouted swung a lanthorn. He was calling to the royally-garbed women, the tiger-cloaked officers, the priests now pouring out of the bow pavilion and lighting the old rowing pits with the glare of their oil lamps and high-borne torches.

The officer in the smaller barge being towed along down on the river's roughening surface cupped one hand and bawled again: "Masters! Lord Hel! Most holy Queen. I beg you to come down and aboard. The water grows worse. We are already far past the ritual debarkation point. I fear..." A curse. The man's hand went out. It caught that of a comrade. Otherwise, the first man would have been pitched into the black roil of Phrixos.

Clustered at the rail near the old oar pit, several of the tiger-cloaked officers hastily began to rig a kind of sling chair to a line. Brak thought he saw a chaplet gleaming against the woman's lustrous hair. Queen Rhea would be the first to leave. The barbarian decided that he would not question her boon. He would go ahead of them all.

He caught hold of one of the torch poles, jumped lithely to the rail.

"Nicor!"

"Nicor!"

"Prince Nicor walks!"

In wave after wave of booming thunder, thousands of voices upon the shore at last articulated their message. The impact struck home to those gathered in the old oar pits, and suddenly there was much shouting, baring of blades. From one knot of men, Lord Hel broke loose. He ordered several of his soldiers forward at the run.

They came boiling back toward the stern, black and yellow cloaks standing out in the wind, swords gleaming sharp. Brak hesitated on the rail. There was a savage fury beating within him that demanded at least one life in repayment for their plotting to use him to dupe a whole kingdom.

A ceremonial spear lay canted across the base of the catafalque Brak had just quitted. He jumped down again, shifted sword hands, snatched up the spear. Grinning cruelly, he waited until the black-shining breastplate of the first of Hel's men rose above the deck level as the man climbed the narrow stair from the oar pits.

Brak cast the spear straight and hard.

The man shrieked, spread eagling in the air. Caught on the stair, he spun and fell with the spear sticking from his chest, and vibrating. His fellows knocked him aside instinctively. The speared man went tumbling off the rail, straight down.

A welter of cries. When Brak looked again, one of Hel's officers had been thrown from the prow of the smaller barge bobbing below. And somehow, the lines that had secured the smaller craft to the great one had parted.

In the space of a breath, the narrow gulf of black water between the two crafts widened. Thus, by one awful stroke of circumstance when the speared man fell, was the escape route cut.

Down in the pits, panicked screaming and cursing broke out.

Sickened, Brak whirled from the rail. His own headstrong rage for revenge had caused the accident. He went into a fighting crouch as the troops of Hel, Lord of the Tigers, regrouped to come charging up the stairs again.

Tall and desperate faced, Hel himself pushed up behind them, beating at them with his fists, crying: "Take him! Take him and carve his damned-of-the-gods bowels from his body! We've no way off this death scow thanks to him. Take him before a single one of you tries to jump and swim!"

A little thicket of blades gleamed as four of Hel's soldiers inched their way along the deck. The barge lurched. It was heading swiftly into the thickening mists. Upon the shores, the thousands howling their fright and fury were almost invisible, their massed torches muted by the blowing dampness to the merest orange flickers. Brak's broadsword flashed up.

He was prepared to stand and kill and die now. Past the charging soldiers, he saw another frightening little vignette: Lord Hel had turned back a moment, found Queen Rhea, and was shaking her violently by the shoulders. Hel bent toward her, berating her as he thrust and knocked her frail body against the makeshift altar.

Had the Lord guessed she had helped him? Brak didn't know, but Rhea hung limp in the Lord's hands, and her face shone in the distance. Fresh tears of fear?

"Attack from the left," snarled one of the tiger-cloaked officers, closing in.

Two others slipped around to come at Brak from the opposite side. Breathing fast, Brak darted backward until he bumped against the catafalque. He scrambled up on top of it, a desperate idea taking wordless shape in his head. The first of the soldiers lunged.

Brak thrust downward hard, then lifted. The man went spinning back, hands at his blood-spouting throat as he fell and kicked his heels while he died. By that time Brak had spun, ripping off the silken tunic so that he could move more freely. The barge tilted again, running faster and faster through a growing roar and rumble of water.

Brak fought for balance, reached high. He grasped the rolled rim of Prince Nicor's great gilt shield.

With a lunge that nearly ripped his arms from their sockets, Brak tore down the immense shield. He staggered under its weight, looping it over his left arm. Atop the swaying catafalque, he started to pivot back to face his enemies, broadsword coming up.

Turning, Brak went rigid.

Rising from the other bier where the body of the dead Queen Joenna still lay was a thin, transparent floating ghost.

Beyond the Queen's phantom shape, the dazed Brak saw the tiger-cloaked soldiers warily closing in.

Could they not see it? See her? Could they not see her ghostly coal eyes burning toward him? Hear the weird, ethereal voice keening above the shouts, the cursing, the rumble of water?

"Beloved...*beloved*? I slept at peace until I felt you near and moving. And now the shield is gone, and you leave, I cannot have you go, beloved. We must enter the Dark Veils together. *Together...*

And a ghostly hand reached out and closed on Brak's right forearm.

The gigantic barbarian saw with stunned shock that where the phantom hand gripped, his flesh turned to purple slime. Through his whole body, there was a sudden, all-consuming cold. A cold of the tomb, a cold of frozen eons, a cold of death's soul calling and pulling at him, taking the life from him.

He tried to lift the broadsword, tried to drive the blade through the queen's shade. But his fighting arm was powerless, heavy, immobile in that awful, fleshless clutch.

Closer she floated.... *Closer.*

Brak's right arm purpled wetly beneath its already sickening tint of embalmer's whiting. Now the tiger-cloaked soldiers began to slip in for the final attack. Thrusting up through them came Lord Hel, his pale, sickly face distorted with frustration and fury.

Brak saw it all dimly. Reeling, writhing, trying to drag away from the ghostly touch of the dead queen's fingers, he felt some dim sensibility within him say that the soldiers could not see her. To them, he must look like a man possessed as he jerked and twisted. Lord Hel's boots hammered as he ran.

"Take him! Lay on him! Give him iron through his back, you scum!"

"'Tis the holy sickness," one tiger-cloaked officer shrieked back. "Look at him twist and arch like he's become a devil's thing."

Hel's black gauntlet smashed the side of the head of the tiger-cloaked fighter who had protested. The man's nose ran with red pump. "Will you all defy me?" Hel screamed. "Take him, holy sickness or no. You, Phidor! Gut him, you're nearest!"

All this came to Brak as through a series of shifting, wind-whipped silks, beyond which everything was unreal. The true, terrible reality was the ghostly voice and shape of the dead queen swirling closer.

"I will not let you go from me. *I will not.*"

The eerie cadences hammered inside his head. Somehow, the ghost seemed to have a hundred hands to touch Brak's shoulder, touch his face, touch his leg, freeze him, with the ice of death.

"Strike, Phidor, strike!" Hel shrieked above the wind.

Tiger cloak flapping, the soldier thrust several of his fellows aside and drove his bright blade at Brak's naked ribs.

The yellow-headed barbarian saw the weapon only as a glitter of light in one corner of his eye. He gave another violent wrench to escape the shade's grip. That surge threw him to the side, made the thrust miss when otherwise it might have slid true into his vitals.

The fore half of the attacker's blade seemed to disappear in fogginess. The tiger-cloaked officer staggered back, dropping the sword as he clenched his teeth in unbearable pain. Then, as in a distorted glass, Brak saw that the man's skin was running and dripping like purple pond scum.

The man bit his own hand and ran to the rail. He hung there, mouth foaming, howling like a rabid dog.

Never had Brak fought a stranger duel than the one he fought then.

One dim part of his mind told him he must watch and be wary of the dozen glittering blades to his left and behind him, where the soldiers clogged the deckway under the rows of ivory torches. He knew why they hung back. To them, he appeared to be wrenching, capering, jerking like a madman in frenzy. But he had to fight his greatest battle with the queen's grisly shadow.

The face of Queen Joenna swam closer. Through it Brak saw torches, mist, the barge, all fading as though in a dream. The sad, lonely ghost-eyes seemed to swell, congeal, take on added reality, until Brak felt that he was wrapped in a swirl of pearl mist, felt himself growing sluggish. His body was stiff and unworking. His mind screamed alarm. And still the lips of the queen came toward him, only a moment away from touching his mouth and draining the last little life from his forever.

More dim shouts among the tiger cloaks. Their faces were insubstantial as the ivory-poled torches standing out obliquely above them.

"Lord," one man shouted, "'tis sure slaughter to touch him."

"And slaughter if you don't by my hand!" Hel screamed back, knocking his way to the head of the gang. "A bunch of milk-sucking weanlings." The Lord's unhealthy face blurred in the torch glare, as his mouth spat filthy curses. "I'll put the iron through him. Then, stand out of my way!"

One tiger cloak stumbled directly in front of Hel. The soldier's feet tangled, and he went down. The Lord booted him in the face and blood spurted from the man's eye-socket.

With superhuman concentration, Brak tried to be wary of the sword that was shining bright, now that Lord Hel had whipped it from its ornamented case. Yet the queen's shade was wrapping round and round Brak so that all his bronzed skin turned blotchy, purpled, and began to glisten wet beneath the funeral-white paste.

As Lord Hel slipped in for the kill, Brak saw again what he had seen in the stable of the net.

The flat of the Lord's long, wicked blade was marked half its length with some dead enemy's blackened blood.

In a moment of frightening lucidity, as if all his senses were enlarged, Brak thought he detected tiny silver gleams among the patches of the bloodstain. Silver-wire marks from an armorer's wheel that had ground and ground, to polish off the blood, but had not done the job completely.

"Beloved, beloved, beloved," keened the dead queen.

Then Lord Hel threw his entire maddened strength into the lunge. Like a stab of silver fire, his blade rammed straight and true at Brak's wide back.

I am not Nicor, Brak was trying to force his clogged tongue to shout at the clutching wraith. *I am not.* He was voiceless, voiceless.

He tried to think each syllable. The effort nearly split his skull with pain.

I am not Nicor.

As if time were suspended so that Brak might savor agony forever, Hel's blade seemed to float, blinding bright except where it was blood marked. Vainly Brak struggled to duck downward and away. The queen's wraith dragged on him, shrilling inside his mind with an intensity that was like a dagger slipped between his brain lobes.

"Beloved, the Dark Veils wait—"

The ghostly voice was soft thunder, sweet roaring, filling his mind and body. She was touching him in a hundred places, moving against him and through him because she was a dead soul reaching out to pull his own soul into hers.

Temples beating so hard he thought they would burst, Brak the barbarian drew back his head, choked out a great, broken yell: *"I AM NOT PRINCE NICOR!"*

The barge lifted, lifted high in the stern, and the night was full of screams.

Experiencing the sensation of lift, Brak saw clouds go whipping among torches. The River Phrixos roared.

The barge had swept into limitless murk, into the heart of the Dark Veils, and it was running now on a black, foaming tide. All this sank home in the heartbeat in which Brak saw the blade of Lord Hel sliding at his neck, the direction of the stab altered suddenly by the heaving of the barge. Time which had slowed so agonizingly began to run again, too fast and frighteningly. With one last, tortured spasm Brak threw himself backward away from the dead queen's shade and cried, "I—am—not—Prince—"

Thunderclap! Thunderclap! *Thunderclap! THUNDERCLAP!*

The night was a maelstrom of shattering noise. Through it, Brak heard an awful, sepulchral voice complete the sentence he had begun: "*—NICOR—*"

Twisting his head, Brak saw Lord Hel's face but a hand's width from his own. Hel's eyes bulged like peeled grapes. His sword thrust had missed by a slim margin, plunged into the darkness. There, so bright Brak had to shield his eyes or go blind, the blood marks on Hel's sword were glowing like fire writing out of the darkness.

The voice out of thunder drummed, *NICOR, NICOR, NICOR, NICOR.*

A puff, a flash, a whirl of light...

Something pearlescent and tangible seemed to billow and rise from Hel's blade half hidden in the mist of the queen's shade. Hel tried to let go the haft. He was powerless to do so. His whole body twitched and trembled.

...*NICOR, NICOR*... thundered the billowing murk spouting from the blood marks on the blade. Brak saw his own right arm whitening. The purple melted off, disappearing. In that desperate moment, as Hel stood with his lunge completed but unable to draw back the bloodied blade, from which he had been unable to scour certain stains, Brak understood: *"Murderer!"*

Brak bellowed it again. "Murderer!" He was able now to move enough to sling his left arm free of the shield loops. "*There* is Nicor, all that's left of him. A stain on your sword." Brak gulped air, laughing wildly as he grappled both hands on the haft of his broadsword, raised it over his head and shouted again, *"Murderer!"*

The tiger-cloaked officers sensed the threat. They leaped in, three blades like a little iron forest aimed at the barbarian's exposed belly. Brak kept shouting, "Murderer, murderer of your own prince! So you might take Rhea and the throne *you killed him!*"

Brak brought his broadsword down full, and split Hel's skull to red and gray ruin.

The transformation was instantaneous.

The wraith of Queen Joenna lost form and substance. It began to blend, coalesce, form a whirling cloud that was part the dead queen's soul-stuff, part the awful, haunted ghost-stuff that had come pulsing out of Nicor's blood left on the sword of Lord Hel.

The cloud grew larger, spiraling up and up as the barge began to lurch even more ferociously. Great crashing crests of water broke over the rails. Brak leaped high to the top of the bier. From there he began to chop the broadsword back and forth through the air, lopping off heads and arms of the attacking soldiers.

One of their weapons gashed open his calf. Soon he was standing in a pool of his own running blood, slipping, sliding, struggling for balance as he rammed the broadsword through the garments and breastbone of the attacker who had cut him.

He jerked the blade free with a sickening crunch of wrecked bone. His wild braid flew in the wind behind him. Suddenly he was forced to his knees by the power of the wind that filled all the night, the wind that marked the passing, the uprushing, of the soul-stuff of the dead queen comingled in a whirling pillar of cloud with the soul-stuff of the murdered Nicor. That soul-stuff had been some preternatural life force that had somehow lived on within the blood clot that could not be polished from Lord Hel's iron until vengeance was taken.

Below him, clustering around the bier, the tiger-cloaked soldiers thrust and hacked at his legs. Brak lopped off a head. Then he cut downward and did the same to an arm. But his mind was haunted, bemused. He wondered if death were near. He could think only, *A soul out of a sword... Nicor's soul. His body was butchered but his soul remained, until Joenna found it, touched it, set it free, seeing at last that I was not Nicor at all.*

The strange thoughts reverberated in his mind like a chant as he fought. Blood bath followed blood bath, corpse piled on corpse as Brak fought off the tiger cloaks. The barge raced faster. The silken pavilion hangings were shredding away, blowing off into the wind-whipped mist. Black-shining boulder cliffs loomed on either side. The barge was rushing down a dark gorge.

Brak slit the cheek of another attacker, stamped down upon yet another's hand as it crawled in to grab his naked foot where it was planted on the gore-running bier. Then the big barbarian recognized a different sort of thunder in the blowing darkness ahead.

This paradise for the people of Phrixos was only a fog-shrouded gorge where the great river plunged fast over foam-bubbling rapids and, if his ears were still functioning aright, crashed over a gargantuan falls.

Brak knew his assessment was true when the barge gave another lurch, struck a rock, and nearly went over on its rail. A great smashing wave extinguished all the torches and snapped the ivory poles to port. The last few tiger cloaks gave up and went for the rail, leaping wide, disappearing into the foaming water with demoniacal howls of fright.

"Barbarian? Barbarian! The lights are gone, *where are you?*"

Above the roar of the wind and water, above the shrieking of priests and sycophants flinging themselves off the doomed craft as it plunged toylike through increasingly rough rapids, Brak heard the thin voice crying out. His lungs ached as he shouted back:

"Here, my lady! Queen Rhea, here! On the stern in the dark. Cling to the rail and beware of the dead men sliding."

"I'm afraid. We have passed the Dark Veils."

"I see you," Brak shouted, though in truth he barely could see at all. Foam-cresting waves threatened to knock him from his slippery perch on the bier. A seething luminous comber went washing past him as he kneeled and held on, searching the dark for Queen Rhea.

A few starboard torches still managed to flicker in the wind and roar. By their light, Brak saw a frightful apparition. A woman with breasts of gold blared vengefully out of the dark at him her horns ashine.

The shield!

"This way! Follow my voice, my lady. This way!"

Brak's throat was growing blood raw as he bent over to grapple for the great shield before it washed overboard. It was a prize he knew he must save, even as he tried to save himself and the queen, who appeared suddenly, servant's cowl sodden at her shoulders. She lurched past the corpses littering the deck and fell panting against the edge of the bier.

"We have blasphemed, blasphemed," she moaned, rolling her head side to side.

"Girl, stop your maundering and hang onto my arm," Brak panted. He clambered down from the bier

and caught Rhea in his arms as another ferocious tilt
of the barge plunged them both against the rail with
brutal, bone-hurting impact. The barge was twisting
round and round like a cork in the blackness. The roar
of the falls was deafening.

Rhea sobbed, kicked at him, scratched, terrified:
"We have angered the Horned Lady! We have entered
paradise alive. We deserve—"

Furiously, Brak knotted his fist in her hair and
yanked her head back until she trembled under his
baleful gaze. "Girl!" he thundered. "We will die,
deserving or not, unless we get overside. This paradise
of Phrixos is a falls without bottom. Now hang on
to me!"

And, with his strength ebbing, he gathered her up
within the crook of his left arm, from which the shield
now hung. Slamming his broadsword back into place,
he used his right hand to grasp one of the ivory poles
and drag himself up on the rail with his double burden.

Then, nothing but seething wet thunder below,
he leaped.

The maelstrom caught them and tossed them. It battered Brak's brains into such dullness and confusion
that, later, when he came back to his senses with his
gashed leg still throbbing, he did not know how they
had gotten to the place where they clung precariously.

The temporary sanctuary was a great, black piece
of hump-backed granite, one of several thrusting up
at the point where the rapids foamed most furiously,
just before River Phrixos plunged into a falls whose
nether depths, fathomless, were hung with slowly
coiling mist.

Now Brak remembered a shattering impact, as if a
wave had flung them against the stone. He discovered
that he was bloody from fingertips to elbows, even
with the river laving him.

He looked down at Queen Rhea damp and huddled against his gigantic chest. Somehow he knew that they had clung to the rock all the long night. The dull, hazy white light of morning filtered down through the swirling fog.

"I'd guess this is all the daylight we'll get in this forlorn place," Brak panted. He scanned the rapids. It would be a long, cruel clamber. But they had no choice. "My lady? My lady, we must…"

Through cracked lips, Brak suddenly made a sound that was supposed to be a self-mocking laugh. He'd remembered that at the moment when they had been closest to death aboard the barge, he had stripped away pretense and screamed at her as *Girl*.

"Girl? Listen."

"The Horned Lady will destroy us," Rhea mumbled, delirious. "We have profaned."

"It was the Tiger Lord who did the profaning," Brak gasped. "He slew Nicor on the battlefield and destroyed his body, hoping that, through you, he would gain the throne. But he couldn't destroy Nicor's soul. It lived on."

The barbarian's voice faded. He had been prattling to himself. She could neither hear nor comprehend, she was so frightened.

Silently Brak held her and marveled. He had seen many wonders, awful beasts and magical feats in his long journeying. But never before had he known of a love as strong as that of the dead Queen Joenna for Nicor. It was a love that had ranged past death, and kept her soul searching, until she found his soul also, or all that was left of it, prisoned in its slayer's sword. Brak doubted he would ever be able to forget the sight of that swirling pillar of cloud rising from the barge, two souls liberated to whatever paradise their own gods arranged.

Another wave crashed and drained down Brak's back. He looked down at the sorry, bedraggled but somehow lovely creature shuddering in the crook of his arm and the scant cover of the battered gilt shield. He felt chilled, weary, almost beyond caring. But the girl's face stirred him strangely.

"After all," he said (or perhaps he only thought) "remember—she is the Queen."

Thus Brak found strength to begin, and eventually complete, the slow and torturous creep over wave-battered rocks. He brought them exhausted and alive to the rocky and mist-hung shore.

There the big barbarian sank down upon his arms while the shield rolled away and the icy river spray pelted him. His mind drained to black emptiness.

Leagues to the southward, Brak the barbarian sat on a new, blooded pony at the fringe of a fig grove overlooking the spires and gilt-leafed onion domes of a great city to which he and Queen Rhea had found their bedraggled way.

Considerable time had passed since their arrival. One harvest had ripened to the full. Brak had led them to the city for a purpose, counseling Rhea against returning to Phrixos until the time was propitious. He had reminded her in his own rough fashion of the thousands who had stood on the shores that haunted night when the barge entered what was supposed to be paradise.

The watchers had seen what they thought was the corpse of Nicor rise and fight. Thus, if Queen Rhea were to rule, she must rule with a sign and symbol of her coming that was far more powerful than any bad omens the priests might read into the barge's strange passing.

Together, they had hatched and plotted such a sign and symbol.

For six waxes and wanes of the moon, Brak had bonded himself into one of the dust-choking granite quarries lying outside this great kingdom-city, which was famed for its figs and cut stone. He and Rhea had taken a poor upper chamber in a bad quarter. They had slept on pallets with a straw screen between them, and lived all the months much like brother and sister, untouched and untouching, although several times, on nights when his mighty back ached from hours of work with the quarry-hammers in the broiling sun, Brak had yearned to speak to her.

He had not. For he knew if he did, his words would put him forever in bondage.

Yet he owed Queen Rhea the debt of his life. And for that reason, he suffered the ten-thonged whips of the quarry overseers on his back. He suffered the insults of the ragtag workers who spat on him and jeered at his barbaric ways and mien. Weekly he and Rhea would add a tiny pile of glittering dinshas to those already in the hide pouch she guarded both night and day.

Finally there was enough.

More weeks had passed while the metalsmiths labored. Brak slept in their shop, dozing with broadsword across his thighs in a comer, so that there might be no chicanery. Lastly, he and the girl had visited a caravanseri, there hiring two dromedaries and one disreputable-looking but reputedly trustworthy trailman. This fellow waited now a short way off, near the edge of the fig grove'. Meditatively the man scratched fleas upon the flanks of his beasts and upon his own raffish person.

Around her dark hair, Rhea had drawn a simple, sky-blue veil. Her gown was linen, poor stuff, but new and clean. Het eyes were brightened by the sundown flash from the busy city's gilded and silvered onion domes. To Brak she was heartbreakingly beautiful.

"Brak, there are no words…" she began.

"None can suffice anyway," he said gruffly. He hid his hurt behind a rough smile. Beneath him, the pony stirred to be away. "What you gave me was life'. What I gave you is less. Only a metal thing."

Unslinging it from where it gleamed across his back, he passed it across to her. The weight of the great gilt shield caused her to gasp a little, but she managed to hold it.

"Remember," he cautioned, "tell them nothing, save that you were borne into paradise beyond the Dark Veils, but have returned to rule. Present them with the sign that your goddess, the Horned Lady, protected you from death and thus finds favor in your rule. The sign will convince them."

Brak's huge, powerful hand pointed to the surface of the great shield. It gleamed free of dents now. In the red light of evening, the Horned Lady looked out warlike at the world, her dagger on its chain between her breasts, her lightning fork and sheaf upheld in either hand. But the metalsmiths had worked a clever artifice upon he face of the goddess. It was a trick that had occurred to Brak upon remembering the coin Lord Hel had twinkled under the net.

On the shield, the Horned Lady's face was now that of Rhea in every detail.

The girl touched his forearm. A tear gleamed on her cheek. Brak stiffened. This was pain worse than any he had ever known in battle.

"Brak, ride north with me. Together, we…

Brak's smile was heavy in the silence. "But Khurdisan is south."

"Those months in the quarry, they were unbearable for you, weren't they?"

"I owed them to you, and more," he replied, though her comment was tellingly true.

"You... you must go on to the south?"

"Yes, Khurdisan lies there, Rh—my lady. That is where I must go."

"Surely that is a terrible road for a man like you to follow, full of perils."

"Yes, that's so." For a moment Brak's memory was haunted by a vision of the dark-molten eyes of Ariane, and of the crawling face of Septegundus, the Amyr of Evil upon Earth. Septegundus would never forget. Septegundus knew that Brak was bound for Khurdisan, and one day he would bar the way with horrors past imagining. *I will be there*, said Septegundus in the Ice-marches. Yet Brak would not turn aside. "I must go on, that's all," he repeated in a low voice.

"Why?" It was softly said, and pleading.

"If I knew that for certain," he said slowly, thinking it out

aloud, "why, then, I would not have to go. Partly I must go there because I was cast out by my own people. Partly I must go there because the tales of Khurdisan burned inside my head from the moment I heard them. But the greatest reason is something I don't even understand myself—call it the working of the fates. It says that my road lies that way, and there's no point in questioning."

Abruptly she clung to him. She kissed his great corded neck. The trailman soothed his dromedaries, whose bells were tinkling. The man coughed with great loudness.

"Then ride to Phrixos when you return," Rhea whispered. "Even if it is ten years from now. Or a hundred. There will be but one woman on the throne, and no man. No man, ever—unless you ride back."

"Perhaps I will. But it would be a long way. And I..."

So wrought with emotion was the big barbarian, he was forced to alter his tone, speak out almost as though issuing a command: "My lady, the trailman is anxious to be away. The light is failing. Take the shield and rule well. Goodbye."

"Brak!"

She ran a few paces after him as he jingled off through the rustling fig trees. Her voice was sweet witchery, but he did not turn toward her even for an instant. He did not dare.

Then, when finally he reached the base of the grove's hill, he risked a backward look at last. She and the driver and the dromedaries were gone from the sullen sundown-lit crest. The grove was empty.

He reached down to pat the warm neck of his pony. "I hope you're fleet, my friend. Time's been lost. And almost more than time, too. For I'll tell you though I'd tell no one else, I could have gone with her. I almost did. Well, enough."

So saying, the barbarian rode ahead to the traffic-laden highway, and back into the hurly-burly of the great city, where he immediately set about asking directions to the best highroads into the far-lying south.

About the Author

New York Times best-selling author John Jakes created Brak the Barbarian for a tale published in *Fantastic Stories* (March 1965). The collected Brak tales later appeared in five volumes, beginning with *Brak the Barbarian* in 1968.

Jakes also is the creator of the eight-volume *Kent Family Chronicles*, the Main and Hazard families of *The North and South Trilogy*, and the Crowns of Chicago, German-Americans whose stories interweave the history of the twentieth century in *Homeland* and its sequel, *American Dreams*. His 2002 novel, *Charleston*, returned him to the turbulent years of the Revolution and the Civil War, and became his sixteenth consecutive *New York Times* bestseller.

Until its demise in the 1980s, Jakes was a member of the Swordsmen and Sorcerers' Guild of America (SAGA) whose other members included Poul Anderson, L. Sprague de Camp, Fritz Leiber, and Michael Moorcock.